W·P· Kinsella

·RED·
·WOLF·
·RED·
·WOLF·

SOUTHERN METHODIST UNIVERSITY PRESS
DALLAS

Published by arrangement with Harper Collins Publishers Ltd., Toronto
First Southern Methodist University Press edition, 1990

Library of Congress Cataloging-in-Publication Data

Kinsella, W. P.
    Red wolf, red wolf / W.P. Kinsella. — 1st Southern Methodist
University Press ed.
        p.   cm.
    ISBN 0-87074-319-8 (cloth). — ISBN 0-87074-314-7 (pbk.)
    I. Title.
PR9199.3.K443R43   1990
813'.54—dc20   90-52661
                                                                    CIP

Printed in the United States of America

TABLE OF CONTENTS

For my friend Kay Harper,
the sister I never had –
thank goodness.

KNOCKS AT THE DOOR
A STRANGER

Baba Drobney, my Yugoslavian grandmother, used to tell me stories. I
was an only child, raised on an isolated homestead in Northern Alberta
in the late 30s and early 40s. My parents, though neither had been
beyond grade eight, were readers, and they, together with my Aunt
Margaret who lived with us, read aloud to me a great deal. Baba
Drobney, who did not read English, was the storyteller and oral
historian of the family. Since I had no children to play with – the nearest
family with children lived several miles away – until I was 10 years old
and moved to the city, I thought I was a small adult. I created my own
fictional friends and made up stories about them. Sometimes in the
evening Baba Drobney and I swapped stories, she setting hers in her
native Yugoslavia, in the hills near Dubrovnik, where she grew up, the
seventh and final daughter of a wine merchant, while I set mine in the
only place I knew, rural Alberta.

Baba Drobney knew the art of storytelling. She would begin by
describing the farm or village home of the main character. Whether the
hero of the story was Josef the shepherd's son, or Katrinka the cheese-
maker's daughter, Baba Drobney set her scene carefully: Josef or Katrinka
would, at the end of the day, be sitting at the table, perhaps a tasty soup
bubbled in a cauldron over the hearth fire. Everything was at peace, the
world unfolding as it should. "And then," Baba Drobney would say,
springing the trap, "knocks at the door a stranger."

From that moment the story leapt forward, whether the caller was a
neighbor, a priest, a prince, a pedlar, a soldier, a band of Gypsies, a
spirit, or a talking animal, their arrival forever changed the life of Josef or
Katrinka.

Until I came to write this introduction I hadn't consciously thought of
Baba Drobney's tales for many years, and I had no idea how indebted I
was to her until I set out to introduce the title story "Red Wolf, Red

Wolf." The first thing I discovered was that the story begins with a stranger, Enoch Emery, knocking on the door of author Flannery O'Connor.

"Red Wolf, Red Wolf" came about because of my admiration for Flannery O'Connor, probably the best short fiction writer the United States has ever produced. A few years ago fellow writers Merna Summers, W.D. Valgardson and I formed a loosely organized group called The Enoch Emery Society. The only requirement for membership was an admiration for the writing of Flannery O'Connor (enforced), and a promise to, once a year, dress up in a gorilla suit and go around shaking hands with people (not enforced). I have for many years listed The Enoch Emery Society on my resume, and it appears in various directories and Who's Who, world wide.

Enoch Emery was a terminally lonely young man in O'Connor's story "Enoch and the Gorilla," which was later incorporated into her novel *Wise Blood*. In the story, Enoch sees people lined up in front of a theater to shake hands with a man in a gorilla suit, The Great Gonzo, and he decides the way to popularity is to dress like a gorilla. After The Great Gonzo insults him, Enoch steals the gorilla suit and is last seen standing at the side of a road puzzled and disbelieving, after frightening off a couple of young lovers by offering to shake hands.

Looking over the more than 200 short stories I have written, the complication of a stranger suddenly appearing in the main character's life, and altering that life forever, happens with great frequency. Baba Drobney taught me more than I ever realized.

In "Evangeline's Mother," Henry Vold first has the teenage daughter he hardly knows thrust on his doorstep, then her friend Evangeline appears, and finally Evangeline's mother, the combination ultimately changing Henry's life forever. In "Driving Patterns" a young woman's brief encounter with a stranger colors the rest of her life.

In "Lieberman in Love" Lieberman is the stranger who appears at the office of a female rental agent, he is also the stranger who picks up a prostitute on a downtown street, his relationships with the two women forever altering his life. "Elvis Bound" is a story where life imitates art. Elvis Presley is the stranger who disrupts the love life of a ballplayer and his wife, a woman who may or may not be Elvis' daughter. While my story was written in 1984-85, there is currently a woman grabbing headlines by claiming to be the E-man's secret daughter.

"Billy in Trinidad" is a story where Billy the Kid is one of the strangers who alters the life of a former Wells-Fargo clerk in Trinidad, Colorado, in 1880. In the story that is my favorite, "Mother Tucker's Yellow Duck," a young man meets a stranger in a park, a sweet, undemanding woman, who, in the spirit of W.B. Yeats' *Cathleen ni Houlihan*, represents the essence of a generation, for the story is my farewell to the 60s, the most exhilarating decade I have lived in. Glorianna and Mac live an idyllic life until Mac, unable to enjoy paradise, lets another stranger rearrange his life.

I was fielding questions after a reading recently when I mentioned getting an idea for a story. Someone in the audience asked me to define "Getting." How did I come up with ideas? they wanted to know.

Glancing at the stories in the book I can see where most originated. "Red Wolf, Red Wolf" for instance, was probably influenced by Pirandello's play *Six Characters in Search of an Author*, since I begin the story by having a fictional character confront the author who created him.

"Truth and History" was, I'm sure, influenced by another Pirandello play, *Right You Are If You Think You Are*. The idea that there can be two or more perfectly logical explanations for an event has always intrigued me. "Butterfly Winter" came about because I watched a documentary on the Monarch butterfly, and I hope it will be a chapter in a future novel.

I use little autobiography in my fiction; I always maintain that my life is too dull to write about. Consequently, the stories that interest me least are "Apartheid," and "For Zoltan, Who Sings," because each contains some autobiography, or are based in part on incidents in my life. I once traveled to a mental hospital outside Boston to rescue a friend who had a breakdown while on a business trip. In "Zoltan" I catalogued much of my friend's story. Zoltan existed, and did indeed sing several times a day in an exotic foreign language. "Apartheid" is much angrier than I usually let my stories get as I tried to recount fictionally my frustrations in dealing with petty and insensitive academics.

"Lieberman in Love" was precipitated because I saw a hooker eating a cookie in front of a Mrs. Field's Cookie Store on Kaiulani Avenue in

Honolulu, while earlier the same day I had encountered a very beautiful rental agent. I had no contact with the hooker and probably spent three minutes with the rental agent, but I wanted to write about both – that is the wonderful thing about being a fiction writer, I simply kept the images in my mind but invented all the details. "Oh, Marley" came about because I read an article in a *National Enquirer*-type magazine about a very large woman who was stabbed numerous times but suffered no serious injury. I wanted to imagine how that incident affected her life.

The first germ of "Billy in Trinidad" originated when I read a small, privately printed collection of reminiscences of old people living in a nursing home in El Paso, Texas. One of the women mentioned that when she was a young girl, Billy the Kid had lived in her father's rooming house in Trinidad, Colorado. By coincidence my wife has relatives in Trinidad, Colorado. We visited there in the fall of 1985. Though there are rumors of Billy the Kid spending time there, none are confirmable, but I did find some interesting history to weave into the story. Sister Blandina was a real person who in her retirement years wrote her memoirs, and the Purgatory River, and Fisher's Peak exist today.

I didn't realize that I was already serving my apprenticeship as a writer, when, long years ago, by the light of the coal oil lamp and the heat of the kitchen wood stove, Baba Drobney would balance me on her ample knee and begin, "Jaroslaw the tailor was the richest man in our village. He was sitting at his table, drinking tea with honey and goat's milk in it and watching the sun set. He had a beautiful wife, a son who he hoped would follow in his trade. Jaroslaw was counting his blessings and was content. Then, knocks at the door a stranger..."

W. P. Kinsella
White Rock, B.C.
May 5, 1987

RED WOLF, RED WOLF

> . . . *we make things up and then they happen.*
> – Jane Burroway

Milledgeville, Georgia. 1983.

First of all I want you to know that I amounted to something in my life, just like I always knew I would. I was created from tough stock. None tougher. She was doing what she did right up until the day she died. And I reckon I will be too. She fought that red wolf who was stealing her life away, fought it with all the strength of her body and her mind.

"I wouldn't ordinarily have thought this possible," is what she said to me, not long after I came to live with her.

"No ma'am," I said. "Not ordinarily. I was created from tough stock, that must have been the reason I come."

"I reckon," she said, but she had her brows creased, her eyes squinted in puzzlement. "Why you?" she went on. "Why not somebody else? *They* were all created from tough stock."

"I think it was because of the way you left me, ma'am. Others you abandoned in predicaments, but none so worse off as me."

"I reckon," she said, but it was easy to see my explanation didn't satisfy her.

1

I knew I'd find her. Animals *do* have instincts. I hoped it would be soon, because I'd been shooed off, screamed at, abused and threatened for quite a few days, ever since I found myself beside that highway, staring across a valley at the skyline of Atlanta, dressed in a gorilla-suit and longing for human contact. On about the tenth day I knocked on the back door of this new-painted farmhouse. A shape appeared behind the screen of the door; they could see me, but I couldn't see them.

"Howdy," I said, sticking out my paw, "I'm just hankering to be friendly."

"Well, I reckon," said a lady's voice. When she pushed open the door I saw she was tall and angular, with reddish hair pulled to the back of her neck, the top of her head hid by a straw sunbonnet. She had small, lively eyes in a long, freckled face. She started to laugh, but then she held it back, for she had seen something in me nobody else had. She realized that no matter what the reason I was on her doorstep, I was serious as could be about it.

"I'm right pleased to meet you, Mr. Gorilla," she said, setting aside that laugh like dumping a dirty dish into a sinkful of suds.

"You got more burrs in your fur than I believe is legal here in the state of Georgia," she went on, grasping my paw with her own solid, long-fingered hand. I noticed that the back of that hand, and what arm was visible outside her long-sleeved blouse, was blotched red. I'd seen me the red wolf for the first time, but I didn't know it then.

"I reckon I'm not in as good a shape as I once was," I volunteered. "I been traveling some."

"I suspect a curry comb would do you a world of good," the lady said, again without a trace of a laugh. Then she surprised me by saying, "What can I do for you, Mr. Gorilla?"

"This is my first time, ma'am," I said, letting go her hand. "Ain't nobody ever been friendly to me before, so I don't rightly know what to do next." I picked up some green foxtail, a piece or two of cinder, and some cotton from out the fur on my belly.

"Well, don't look at me," said the lady. "I've never in my life had a gorilla for a gentleman caller. However," and she smiled, only it was a friendly smile, not a making-fun-of-me smile, "if y'all are housebroken, and if a gorilla drinks coffee, I was just about to have a cup myself."

"I'd thank you kindly for the coffee, ma'am," I said, and I wiped my feet on her rubber-tire doormat that had WELCOME painted on it in white letters.

That's how Miss Regina found us, her daughter and a gorilla sipping coffee at the kitchen table.

"Why Mary Flannery," she said, "I didn't know you had company."

Miss Regina was like that, still is actually; she could walk in to find the President of the United States himself, or a gorilla, sitting at her kitchen table, and she wouldn't let it faze her a jot.

"I do believe I'll have a cup of coffee myself," she said, crossing the room to the stove.

"Mama, Mr. Gorilla here just stopped by for a friendly visit."

"Howdy," I said, and stuck out my hand. And for the second time since I put on the gorilla-suit somebody shook hands with me. Miss Regina's hand was small and soft, but it had a willowy strength to it. Just touching her caused me to tear up and my breath to come short. I was glad the pink celluloid eyes of the gorilla kept the ladies from seeing my tears.

Eventually Miss Regina went about her business, and me and Miss Flannery walked to the yard where she set about tending her peacocks. They was rattlin' and whistling and acting like a parade was passing by, but weren't they beautiful. One fanned his big old tail and it looked like a Chinese screen I seen at a museum I visited once. That fanned tail blinked like it was lit from behind, while dozens of blue and green eyes winked as if they had their own life. I was standing on the edge of the grass all hunched up dark as a cloud inside my gorilla-suit.

"There seems to be an exceptional coincidence afloat," Miss Flannery said to me, as she scattered a handful of grain to the gibbering peacocks. "I've recently had a book published in which I wrote about a boy in a gorilla-suit who was simply dying to shake hands with people." She stared at me squinty-eyed, extending her long neck in an imitation of one of her birds.

"I knew you was the one the minute you opened up your screen door to me," I said, and I burst out with more talk than I aimed at anybody in my entire life, as I told her about travelin' around Georgia searching for days and days for somebody who'd shake my hand. "I was so afraid I wouldn't find you," I ended up.

"Is this a joke?" she asked, pushing her neck further forward, staring my costume right in its pink celluloid eyes.

"I don't know whether you know this or not, ma'am, but when a book gets itself published, why some characters get lives of their own."

"My book's only been out a week," she said, then flushed scarlet at the very idea she might have believed me. "Did my editor hire you?" she asked.

I shook my head.

"My publisher?"

I shook again.

"Some friends of mine? New York? Atlanta?"

"No ma'am."

The peacocks, full of grain, went patty-footing it away. We climbed to the back porch where Miss Flannery sat in the shade on a white-enamelled porch swing, while I leaned on a porch pillar. The swing creaked back and forth.

"If," she said, eyeing me balefully, her lips sealed up like they'd been zippered. "If I believed for one minute what you say is true, then you'd be called Enoch Emery."

"That's right, ma'am."

She laughed in a hearty, genuine way. "I'll be," she said.

"I reckon you will," I replied, holding up my end of the conversation.

"Tell me, Enoch, do *characters* always find the authors who created them?"

"Most of them don't have to," I said, though I wasn't sure how I knew that.

"But you did."

"It was on account of the way you left me, ma'am, abandoned me, if you will. Weren't nobody in the world was going to shake my hand but you. So I *had* to find you."

"A character only an author could love," said Miss Flannery. She stayed silent for a long time, staring me up and down with her jolly, puzzled eyes.

"You permanent?" she finally asked. "What if my book goes out of print. I ain't exactly a famous author."

"Gone," I said."

"Gone where?"

"I don't rightly know, ma'am. To sleep, I reckon. Can't be too bad a place for I don't have a powerful fear of it."

"I don't reckon my book will stay in print more than a few months. You better enjoy yourself while you can."

Over the next few days Miss Flannery helped me to clean myself up some, though I wasn't ready to come out from inside the gorilla-suit.

"I have to admit I don't like the implications," Miss Flannery said. "I don't like them one bit. I don't like the idea that I created you. That you didn't exist until I wrote you down on my typewriter yonder."

"You believe in the supernatural, don't you?" I countered. I knew she did. She had beads and crucifixes and other religious paraphernalia laying about. And her shelf of books. She read books I couldn't even pronounce the titles of, about things like theology and philosophy and psychology.

"I do, indeed," she said. "What troubles me is I'm unsure which side sent you to me," and she looked at me with a squinty, twisted-up smile, but that smile held no malice, never did, never could.

"Maybe I'm one of them *travails* the Bible is so fond of mentioning."

"Maybe you are. Seems like a good word. It was women who mainly suffered travails, and they had mainly to do with sickness and birth, and Lord knows I've had my share of sickness, and now you turning up this way is a birth of sorts."

Miss Flannery always joked about staying one jump ahead of the old red wolf, which was her way of talking about her illness.

"*Lupus* means wolf in Latin," she told me. "Lupus the disease is a kind of T.B. of the skin," and she showed me her hands which had red sores on them, like a bad rash or the eczema. I learned that her daddy had died of the disease and that there wasn't much could be done for it, except stay out of the sunshine and rest a lot.

"The old red wolf she ebbs and flows, some days I'm chipper as a sparrow, on others I sit in front of my typewriter and every finger feels like it weighs five pounds.

"My insides look just like my outsides," she said to me once, extending her poor, red-blotched hand toward me. "That red wolf just plumb tires me out, Enoch. Tires me out. I don't know how much longer I can stay ahead of it." That was the closest to self-pity she ever came in all the years I knew her.

I'd been Miss Flannery's guest for about three weeks, when, one morning over coffee at her sunny kitchen table she said to me, "The thing is, Enoch, what *are* we going to do about you? Do you know what would happen if I turned you out on the road? I don't guess I could be held legally responsible for you. What do you reckon?"

"I don't guess you could," I said. The coffee cup was a tremblin' in my hand when I said that. I knew I'd just wander 'til I died if she turned me away; they'd find this long, thin, starved-to-death gorilla in some small town garbage dump. Much as I wanted to I didn't say anything else. I couldn't bring myself to ask for her mercy, couldn't ever give her a moment of guilt if she decided to get shed of me.

"I wonder if I should let your being here become public knowledge. Do I claim you as a relative? I can just see me saying to some of the church women who come to call, 'This here's Enoch. I wrote him and he come to life.'"

I felt truly fearful at that moment.

"I reckon there must be somethin' I could do to earn my keep. I have to admit I'm not dumb," I said. "It ain't like I haven't been to school. I remember I was right smart when it came to describing some place I'd like to visit, which was the city of Atlanta, which is what Teacher asked us to do in fourth grade.

"I was mighty quick at ciphering too. It was just that we got moved off from one farm to another a couple of times each year, and what with my daddy being a convict and all. After fourth grade papa he didn't see much use for me to go to school regular except when the law threatened. Papa could print his name when he had a declaration to sign at the Ordinary's Office, I seen him do it. 'No need for you to have more learning than your old man,' was what he said to me.

"Of course there was that Bible School I went to. Academy was how the Rev. General Bucephalus Jones described it. God's own little angel-soldiers of holy light was what the Rev. General Jones called us. We had angel wings on the shoulders of our tunics. 'Those who are pure in spirit will fly through the air with the greatest of ease,' the Rev. General told us. Couple of boys who thought they were pure in spirit leapt from the top of the guard tower, and another boy tried it from the third floor of the dormitory, but all they got for their troubles were compound fractures, and the dormitory jumper, name of Bond Chute, ended up in wheelchair, head lolling, drool running out the corners of his mouth."

"Nobody says you're dumb, Enoch. But you are a secret, and going to have to stay that way as far as I can see."

"I don't mind bein' a secret," I said. "I'm too shy. I can't go out *there,"* and I pointed toward the highway and the world. "Not unless I was on the sneak. I can't live in *their* world. I can only live in yours."

"Well, shy ain't the end of the world," Miss Flannery said. "We just got to find you something to do with your life where shy don't matter a crumb." She smiled at me, her mouth all twisty with serious thought.

"I'm shy too," she said. She let it go at that. But years later, when both traveling and the old red wolf were taking their toll, she said to me, "Why I'd never leave Andulusa if I had my way. But I have to go out and let folks stare at me occasionally, let them ask dumb questions and make my stories out to be a lot they ain't and never was or ever will be. But it makes them feel smart to put their own interpretations on my stories, and who am I to spoil their fun unless what they say goes to way-beyond-foolish, which it does more often than you'd guess."

"You ain't gonna make me go then?"

"Course not. What we got here is an unusual situation. I just been thinkin' aloud on how to handle it."

I breathed easier than I hardly ever had, and I'm not sure my gorilla face could smile but I sure tried to make it grin, and behind that face my own was smilin' fit to eat a pie at one bite.

"I reckon there's somethin' I could do would make your life more bearable," I said.

"Like what?" said Miss Flannery , eyeing me up and down.

"Like take off my gorilla suit."

"You sure you're ready to do that?"

In answer I undid the six snaps that circled my neck and lifted off my gorilla head.

"Well now," said Miss Flannery, "you look exactly as I described you in my book."

"Can't look no other way," I said.

"That is plumb creepy, Enoch," she said, but she smiled when she said it.

I pulled my arms out of the sleeves and let my long, white hands rest on the table top.

"How do you feel?" she asked. "Do you feel real?"

"Are you my friend?"

"I reckon I am *that* at least."

"Then I feel real as grits. And I feel more relaxed than I ever have. But not enough to go *out there*," I added quickly.

"I'll have to do my best to see you won't have to, Enoch," she said, reaching across the table to hold one of my pale hands.

It was Miss Flannery who found the ad in one of her church magazines. LEARN TAXIDERMY AT HOME IN YOUR SPARE TIME FOR FUN AND PROFIT, was what it said. *Taught by a man of Christian principles, Dr. Horton W. Hathcock, D.D. Veterinarian.* And the ad gave a box number in Rome, Georgia.

I took me that course and I learned to be a taxidermist. I amounted to something, as I always knew I would. Subject matter was a bit of a problem at first. Sometimes in the dead of night I used to sneak out and collect road kills, consequently some of my first work was a little lopsided, and as often as not bug-eyed, but it weren't my fault, and Miss Flannery was quick to acknowledge that.

"You'll do some right good work, Enoch," she said to me, "soon as something dies of its own free will, or we find you a customer."

Finding customers was not easy. Miss Flannery and Miss Regina couldn't suddenly announce an interest in taxidermy and suggest that their church friends bring their own dead pets or their husband's hunting kills over to Andulusa to be stuffed and mounted.

I solved my own problem though, I advertised in the very magazines Dr. Horton W. Hathcock, D.D. Veterinarian, frequented.

TAXIDERMY WORK YOU'LL BE PROUD TO DISPLAY
Leather Tanning
Fur and Hair-On Tanning
Satisfaction Guaranteed
EMERY TAXIDERMY & TANNING
Nearly 30 years experience

The last line was the only lie.

"I figure every ad should be allowed one harmless falsehood," Miss Flannery said, though Miss Regina disapproved. While we was making up that ad Miss Flannery and me laughed like little kids who invent a limited-membership club, with initiations and secret handshakes.

"Pointless giggling," Miss Regina called it.

Miss Flannery arranged a post office box number in Atlanta, and had a brochure printed up that I sent out when I got queries. She also arranged for the contents of the box to be forwarded to Andulusa once a week. Once I had a few satisfied customers I put their testimonials in my ads. I have never met or talked to one of my customers.

These last few years I even teach a bit myself. I made up a correspondence course and advertise it along with my regular ad for the taxidermy business.

What with us both being only children, me bein' an only child twice, if you understand my meaning, I guess we were closer to brother and sister than any other relationship. The years at Andulusa flew by; Miss Flannery wrote her stories while all the while the old red wolf wore her down the way wind erodes open land, slow and easy so's you'd hardly notice, until all of a sudden the top soil is gone and ain't nothing left but twisted roots and rocks.

What does Miss Flannery really think of me? I used to ask myself regular, lying on my single bed in the basement, listening to a country station from Atlanta, smelling the twitchy odors of my tanning chemicals. Miss Regina treats me like I was an ungainly pet. She fusses and complains about the odors my work creates, but then she squeezes my arm and says, "Oh, Enoch, I don't know what we'd do without you."

One afternoon, about my fifth year at Andulusa, Miss Flannery put the shoe on the other foot.

"What do y'all think of me, Enoch?" she asked.

"In what way?" I said, though I knew right well what she had in mind.

"You been a glimpse of God to me," she said. "I look at you and I think I get an inkling of what God must feel when he stares down at His world."

"You know, Miss Flannery, sometimes of an evening when we playin' a game of Chinese checkers or Parcheesi, I steal a glance at you and I feel a little toward you what you must feel toward the God you believe in. I know for a fact you created me. And you're pretty sure He created you. Difference is I got proof."

"And I got all the proof I need. So I reckon we'll stick to Chinese checkers from here on."

And we did. Though I sure did worry some about what would happen to me after Miss Flannery was gone.

"The old red wolf is closing in on me, Enoch," she said to me the last time I saw her.

Miss Regina had come out of the bedroom a few minutes before and said, "Mary Flannery wants a word with you." Miss Regina was pale and worried and I'd heard her on the telephone an hour before making arrangements with the hospital.

I crept into the bedroom, walking careful as if I was stepping on Miss Regina's best china.

"For goodness sakes, Enoch, I ain't dead and gone yet. You don't need to pussyfoot." But she was too weak to raise her head from the pillow when she said it. Though she did force a smile.

"I think it would be plumb criminal if you were to die soon as I do," Miss Flannery said. "I've read about these selfish old kings in Biblical times who had all their wives and all their slaves killed so they could all be together in the hereafter. And I don't care what you think is gonna happen, I won't have no truck with those sort of ideas, let me tell you..."

"Characters can't function in the real world after their creators are dead," I said.

"How do you know?"

"I was created knowing that, ma'am."

"I see," she said. "Well, I think you're wrong, Enoch. We have spent years making you useful. You have harnessed your ambition so as to amount to something. You have an occupation. You'll carry on just fine after I'm gone. See if you don't."

Miss Flannery turned out to be right. Though I don't know what I'm going to do after Miss Regina goes to her reward. Even if the town of Milledgeville, or the university decides to keep this house for a museum, as there is a right lot of talk of them doing, I don't suppose they'll want me. The kind of folks would set up a museum ain't the kind would believe in me anyhow. They'll be shocked and surprised enough just to find that *someone* has been living in this huge old house of Miss Regina's all these years, right in downtown Milledgeville, right under everyone's curious noses.

I think myself that I'd make an excellent custodian. I could wear a uniform, like I did when I worked at the zoo all those years ago. I could act real shy and polite and I could escort little groups of white-haired ladies and long-legged graduate students, each of whom hankers to touch their hands to something of Miss Flannery's, on tours of the house.

We'd have to rope things off so they couldn't touch the furniture, the china, the books. I could explain which things belonged to Miss Flannery, which came originally from Andulusa. And I could tell little stories about her, like how on one of the last days of her life, when she was writing her story "Parker's Back," I found her one morning slicing up an onion with a paring knife, peeling off the brown outer layer, studying it and each further slice she peeled off.

"I just wanted to see if what I thought was true," she said, which didn't explain much to me at the time, but when I read the story I understood.

One time a couple of years ago, I put on a clean shirt, pulled a hat down over my ears, and sneaked out of the house way before dawn. I was at the university when it opened and I gaped just like a tourist at Miss Flannery's bookcases and geegaws that they have on display in a special room. That room has carpeting with peacocks on it, and wouldn't Miss Flannery have loved it though.

Miss Regina just shakes her head in wonder at all the tourists that come to Milledgeville to gawk and to study about her daughter as if what she wrote was Gospel.

"I tell you, Enoch," she said more than once, "up at that room at the university there will be a whole row of small Japanese men in blue suits and striped ties, sitting straight-backed as the chairs they're on, studying Mary Flannery's papers and making notes in upside down-looking writing."

The first time a Japanese edition of one of Miss Flannery's books arrived at the house we both chuckled over it.

"These squiggles run up and down the page," Miss Regina marvelled, "and the book's printed to read back to front."

"It's a wonder to the soul that anyone can read chicken scratchings like that," I said.

I guess my being a caretaker, or even living on here after Miss Regina is gone is more fantasy than reality. Even though I bet I'm the only person alive who knows every nook and cranny of this house, knows its history, which addition was built onto which addition, and when, and by who.

"Me and Enoch sends our love," Miss Flannery one time signed a letter to a close friend. The friend just thought it was a clever joke. She knew literary characters don't come to life.

"How come you don't invent another story about me?" I asked, after I'd been at Andulusa for a few years.

"You're family now, Enoch," she said, "and I never write about family." I think she meant the part about my being family. I was kind of like a kid brother, somebody she could be happy to help out. She was proud of my successes and so was Miss Regina, though she didn't like to say so out loud.

But Miss Regina's glad to have me about now, even though she often says, "Honestly, Enoch, it's like having two shadows, the way I turn around and you're always there."

I believe she thinks of me as a pet; to Miss Regina I'm like one of the animals I preserve and shape and make last forever, a reminder of her daughter, a pet all clear-eyed and slicked down, one that don't cause no trouble by clawing at the curtains or making mayhem with the rugs.

Even with an occupation I know I can't make it out in the real world. I suspect it's because of how I was created. Being a fictional character ain't the easiest of lives. I've kept my gorilla-suit. It's hanging in a closet in the basement, preserved, brushed, and moth balled, in as good a shape as it ever was.

The thought of being on my own is scary though, I could put on the suit and set out to find someone to shake my hand and take me in, which is what I reckon I'll do when I'm thrust out on my own. But as far as I know, Miss Flannery was the only one who was ever going to help me. Ordinary folks ain't partial to hand-shaking gorillas. The one hope I got is that somebody else will write about me. That's possible ain't it? I'll make myself believe it is anyway. I'll set out knocking on doors, searching until I find the new writer. I will. It's worth a try.

SOMETHING TO THINK ABOUT

Mrs. Baron pushes open the screen door and steps out on the verandah of her house, which is tall and square like a five-gallon gas can. The strong, new spring that old John installed on the door in April pulls it shut behind her, with a bang. She walks carefully across the battleship-gray boards and sits down on the porch swing. The swing groans gently.

"Jack? Jack?" she says to attract my attention, though I can tell by the angle of her head that she's staring past me at the acres of July corn that whisper in a feather-like breeze.

"Yes, Mrs. Baron," I say from near the front gate, where I'm tending a bed of snapdragons, some yellow as canaries, others the color of maroon velvet.

"The memorial service is at four o'clock and I won't be there, and neither will John. But I'll give them something to think about. Mrs. Baron will give them something to think about all right. They can push me, but old as I am, I only bend." She pauses, rises from the swing, and comes to the top of the porch stairs. She is wearing beige running shoes, loosely laced, and her swollen feet make ominous bulges in the canvas.

"Do you see this comb?" she says, turning her head so I can just make out the outline of a yellowish comb holding her ermine-white hair in place. "Haven't worn this in a coon's age, I thought this morning. I found it down in the bottom of a dresser drawer. It's ivory; it was part of a set John gave me when we were courting, over 60 years ago."

"It's very nice, Mrs. Baron," I say, not knowing what she may be expecting of me.

The last few days since John died, she's been telling me all sorts of things, keeps having me come back to do work around the yard that I don't ordinarily do. She talks to her daughter, too, as though the daughter could understand everything that was going on. Maybe she considers us a little alike, Missy and me. Missy's mind never grew up, and a lot of people don't think I'm very bright, talk real loud to me when they meet me on the street or in the general store. "Jack Clarke lives all alone in that big old house," they say, "full of books, and he plays the piano late at night. Been to the university, but all he does is odd jobs," and they speculate about what's wrong with me to live the way I do.

"Mrs. Baron, indeed," she says from the top of the steps. "Now it's all right for *you* to call me Mrs. Baron, Jack. But do you know I've gotten to thinking of myself as Mrs. Baron! I wonder how that came about. Sometime in my 60s or 70s, people stopped calling me by my first name and I became Mrs. Baron. Until I was about five, I was called Baby Marylyle. Did you know that? My closest sister was seven years old when I was born. When I was young I was Marylyle McKitteridge. I remember how I labored learning to write and spell a difficult name like that. I used to sit at papa's roll-top desk in Onamata. I'd bite my lips white, and press a stubby pencil into my scribbler, making what my mother used to call sleigh tracks on the paper.

"I remember hearing that name called one time – I won a book prize, a copy of *Little Women*. Was it at school or at church?" She pauses to consider her own question. Ordinarily I'd find some work to do somewhere else on the farm, but I think I should listen to her today. She's had a bad week, Mrs. Baron has; she's just bursting with grief and rage, and she's got to let some of it out. I figure listening is the best thing I can do.

"I remember hearing my name called another time. 'Marylyle McKitteridge,' the voice said, and I walked across the stage of the Onamata Community Hall, not the one that's there now, the one that burned down in 1922, and received my high-school diploma, an ice-blue ribbon around my waist, a homemade corsage of bachelor's buttons on the shoulder of my white satin dress.

"I was in love with John Baron. The bachelor's buttons were for him. 'As blue as your eyes,' I told him later, as I rode home, close by his side on the seat of that tall black buggy. All that humid summer, I worked at the desk in papa's office," and suddenly she smiles, radiantly as if she's looking at a new baby. "And once in a while I'd stop and write versions of my name: Marylyle Baron, Marylyle McKitteridge Baron, Marylyle M. Baron, Mrs. M.M. Baron, Mrs. John Baron.

"And in the fall I became Mrs. John Baron. Over 60 years ago. Now people talk to me as if my Christian name was Mrs., and without noticing, I've accepted it, until it's become part of me, comfortable as an old slipper."

She sits down slowly on the top step, and, like a car changing lanes without signalling, her conversation veers away. "I've got tea inside, Jack, would you have a cup with me?" but she does not wait for a reply. "Father Rafferty would have known what to do. He was a real priest, tall and majestic, his black cassock sweeping the ground, swishing over the grass in time to his long strides, the silver cross at his waist flashing in the sunlight."

She goes on talking about Father Rafferty for a long time. My memories of him are a lot different than hers. I remember an old man, stooped as the crook of a cane, half-blind, half-deaf, his cassock drizzled with food stains. I think there was some controversy about him refusing to retire. About the time I finished high school,

10 or 12 years ago, a big car pulled up at the rectory, which is in Onamata though the church is out of town, and they took Father Rafferty away. It was lunch hour, and we watched a couple of little nuns carry out boxes of his possessions and fit them into the trunk of the car, and a couple of young priests, big as football players, came out one on each side of Father Rafferty, guiding him firmly into the car, his palsied old head bobbing up and down like a baby bird's, his toothless mouth complaining.

"'Rules are not *always* meant to be followed,' he said many times. He used to sit right in there at the kitchen table, playing cribbage with John and sipping dandelion wine. 'Them over there,' and he would wave his hand in whatever direction he thought Rome might be, 'what they don't know doesn't do them the least bit of harm,' and he'd smile, and wink one of his big, blue eyes.

"That new priest is young, and has a face long and bony as a year-old calf. He wears overalls and a checkered workshirt, just like you Jack, and he tries so hard to be one of the people. But all he knows about is following the rules. It doesn't matter a bit how he dresses; it's rules that are important to him, and people come second.

"He at least put on his collar when he came out here and explained to me, over and over, why the rules of the church forbade John being buried in consecrated ground." She turns back toward the door, her feet turned out like a duck's. "Come in, Jack. The tea's on the table."

I follow her through the hall, which is dark with high varnished baseboards, and into the kitchen which still has a tall, black-and-silver cookstove, with a warming oven and a reservoir. The kitchen is spotless, and there's a large window above the table, one that I installed for her a couple of years ago. As we drink tea, we can watch bees droning over her flower garden, which is full of golden marigolds, sweet peas, and cosmos. Close to the house are hollyhocks so tall that their heavy flowers bump against the bottom of the window, like soft fists.

"Mortal sin!" she goes on. "When I was a child, Thaddeus McGreevey died in some state of mortal sin, though I never fully understood what it was that made him an outcast. He was a tiny old man with a whiskey drinker's red face and bleary eyes, who lived in a log cabin, eight or ten miles south of here; it's part of one of those conglomerate farms now, cabin's been gone for 50 years or more. His wife left him, long before I was born. He didn't remarry, that wasn't the problem. Mother used to complain about him taking in an Indian from the Sac-Fox Reservation over by Tama. I saw them together in town. The Indian was fat, with warts on the side of his face, which was big around as a frying pan, and he wore McGreevey's old clothes.

"When McGreevey died, the men of the congregation had a couple of secret meetings that my papa went to but wouldn't talk about. There was even a rumor that the bishop was coming down from Des Moines, but he didn't.

"Finally after all those meetings, they decided to offer McGreevey to the Protestants, and when he told them that McGreevey had left his farm to the Indian and $2,000 to St. Emmerence of Onamata, they told the Catholics to keep him.

"Thaddeus McGreevey was buried outside the cemetery fence in a stone and strangle-grass no-man's land." Her voice breaks. "And they wanted to put my John in the same place."

"I'm sorry, Mrs. Baron. I wish I could be of some help." She seems hardly to hear me.

"Of course, we'll be happy to have a *memorial* service for Mr. Baron,' the young priest told me. 'He was one of the real old-timers around here,' he went on, rubbing his hands together, rattling on, saying a good deal more than he meant, just for the sake of saying something.

"'You do as you like,' I told him. 'John helped build the church when he was a boy,' and as I said that, I could picture John, up on a ladder where he never should have been at his age, applying that coat of cream-colored paint to the steeple. But they have no shame, none of them, they don't take any of that into consideration."

"I don't know much about your religion, Mrs. Baron," I say, "but it seems to me they haven't treated you very fairly."

"When I'm through, they'll remember Mrs. Baron around Onamata for a few years. I'll give them something to think about. Everybody wants to be remembered some way, Jack. Even you, I bet you'd like to be remembered. There was old Dressler. Ha. You must remember him. There I go, talking about him as if his first name was Old. What was it? Norman? No."

"Norville."

"That was it. Thank you, Jack. Sold his farm and moved into the Lions' Club old folks' home in Onamata. They say he got a million dollars when he sold his land, owned two sections he did, and he donated every cent to the University of Iowa Medical Center in Iowa City. They've built something there called the Dressler Pavilion," and she stops to laugh, a harsh, ironic laugh. "Sounds like some place where they'd hold 4-H shows and bake sales.

"Old Dressler sits in an easy chair in his little room and cackles about how part of the University of Iowa is named for him; he must be close to a hundred by now. His kids don't come to see him anymore, since he did that, not even on Christmas or Father's Day. 'Let the medical school send somebody to see him,' one of his daughters said. They got together, the four of them, and hired a lawyer, but he said old Dressler was sane, and if they sued they'd only embarrass themselves."

I smile to myself as I drink my tea. Old Dressler, as she calls him, is a shirt-tail relative of mine. And, for the most part, she has the story correct.

"I'd embarrass myself if I sued. Believe me, I've thought about it. Only, who would I sue? How would I go about suing the Catholic Church? Would I have to sue the pope? Would they have Italian lawyers in red robes? No, even if I had the nerve, it would drag on for years and years. They'd make it drag on knowing that I'd have to die sooner or later. I'm 81 already, a year older than the century, that's how I remember. It doesn't seem possible that I've got a 60-year-old daughter.

"Where is Missy?" I say, maybe to take the conversation away from the church and John, or maybe just to keep her talking.

"Missy's in her room playing with her dolls. Keeps her room real neat, has her jigsaw puzzles stacked up tidy as you please on the shelves John built above her bed. Her and John used to work them puzzles, had one on the go on the dining-room table all winter every winter. And she dresses and undresses her dolls; them Barbie dolls were a godsend and I can whip up them little dresses quick as you please on my sewing machine, and Missy smiles fit to break your heart when she sees a new one. The doctors told us not to expect Missy to live beyond 40 or 45, but she'll be 60 on her next birthday. Has a heart condition, but otherwise she's healthy."

She talks on about how she learned she couldn't have children and how they came to adopt Missy. "John came up from the fields when Doc Spangler dropped us off; Doc drove me into Iowa City and both of us back. John's face was black as an African, with pink holes for his eyes, and I can still see him, the way he peeled back the blanket and peered down at that little pink-apple face – I could just see him fall in love. He carried her like an armful of rose petals and I didn't mind when the field dust rubbed off his shirt onto the blanket.

"At first John was worried that Missy staying a little girl in her mind might have been a punishment heaped on us for going out and getting ourselves a child after God told us we weren't supposed to. John would never hear of adopting another. But we've never been sorry we had Missy. Kids grow up and as soon as they start school, they find out parents aren't gods at all, just dumb farmers, and they keep that attitude until they get out on their own and discover how tough life really is. Missy's been our sweet child for

60 years.

"I don't have anything to explain to Missy. It's nice and it's sad, too, to see the way she acts. I think she realizes that John is dead, but she's able to put it out of her mind. I wish I could. Them last weeks he used to take Missy by the hand and her and him would walk down to St. Emmerence graveyard, there behind the church. I'd watch them and they could have been husband and wife walking off to town, only thing that gave it away was that Missy would skip every once in a while like a little girl, and as they walked she'd be talking so earnestly, up into John's face.

"At the graveyard, John explained real carefully to her that he was going to die in a month or so, and he showed her the spot where he was going to be buried – right next to his papa and mama, and how the spot next to him was reserved for me. The one next to that is for Missy, but he didn't mention that. Sometimes Missy really seems to understand. 'It will prepare her,' is what John said, and I agreed with him.

"Everybody tries to give you the run-around when you're old, Jack. Did you know that?"

"Yes," I say.

"John and I, we had to pry it out of them, the business about how sick he was, I mean. They were all so hopeful, after the exploratory operation, talking about rest and recuperation and how he'd be weak for a few months. 'If you got something to explain, you better say it to me,' John told that doctor. The doctor launched into a new lot of gobbledy-gook. 'You afraid to say cancer, young fellow?' was John's reply. Finally, they told him he had only a month or so left."

"This tea is sort of a bribe, Jack," Mrs. Baron says, looking straight at me. "I never thought I'd get so old I couldn't drive that rattle-trap of a pickup truck, but they took my license away last fall, said my eyesight wasn't good enough. Those flowers I've had you working on don't need nothing done to them that I can't do. All

I've been doing is getting up my nerve for two days, pacing around in here like a coyote in a cage and watching you in the yard doing work I could do."

Mrs. Baron leads the way out to the machine shed, and eventually finds what she wants, which is a long length of aluminum-colored cable, the kind of stuff that was one time used as guy-wires on telephone and power poles. She is wearing a rumpled pair of mauve stretch pants and a blouse the color of owl feathers. Her wrists are no bigger than a child's, and tufts of white hair float around her face as she works, busy as a mother hen.

"Wonder why you don't see guy-wires anymore," Mrs. Baron says as she and I wrestle the cable to the pickup truck and lift it into the back where it wiggles around like a dozen snakes. "Drive me down to the church, Jack," she says, then launches into another story as we drive the mile of gravel road between corn fields.

"'Now Mrs. Baron,' that young priest said, his brown eyes as solemn as a cow's, his hands clasped in his lap. 'I want you to know that it's nothing personal. I don't make the rules,' he said, and looked toward the kitchen ceiling, and there was just the faintest flicker of a smile on his face. Oh, he made me so mad.

"'You're a devout woman, Mrs. Baron,' he said. 'I'm sure you understand the theological implications. But just in case you don't...' and he launched into an explanation that took him all the way back to the time of Christ, and his conversation was splashed full of Latin phrases, like throwing chocolate chips into cookie batter.

"It's funny how people are always ready for change before those in charge. That's why governments are forever being rooted out of office, Jack. And the church would fall the same way, except, long ago, someone was smart enough to invoke the magic of God's name. The poor simply ignore the parts of church doctrine they can't accept. Oh, Jack, it will take the church hundreds of years to catch up to the people."

"I don't know much about matters of religion, Mrs. Baron,"

which is what I imagine she wants to hear.

"The people recognized the foolishness of marriages being made in heaven. Doctrines like that were established when life expec-tancy was about 30 years or less. The same thing with birth control. Young women don't have monstrous families anymore, yet they still attend church. I bet many of them carry their little discs of pills right into church with them – they've decided that *they* are right and the church is wrong, because those doctrines were coined when the world was underpopulated and are no longer logical. But the church fathers backed themselves into a corner by claiming their doctrines were the word of God.

"And now there are women daring to ask for a place in the church – daring to talk about the possibility of women priests, of women being more than producers of children and cooks for church suppers. 'Could anyone know less about women than a group of male celibates?' I read that in a magazine; it didn't mean much to me then, but after what they've done to me and John... 'Somebody has to drag the church into the 20th century,' that article said. I surprised myself by not even arguing with the priest. My chest felt like it was full of fire, like I might explode, but I listened and nodded and sent him away thinking himself a diplomat.

"I had John cremated. Had to send the body to Iowa City, to the Beckman-Jones Funeral Home for that. I picked out an urn, a small one, scarcely bigger than a bottle of aftershave. It's a pleasant blue, a little like John's eyes."

We pull into the churchyard and I begin untangling the cable and removing it from the truck.

"St. Emmerence Church is nearly as old as I am, Jack. A delegation of farmers rode a hundred miles on horseback to Des Moines, and persuaded the bishop to send them a priest. Onamata then was a general store, blacksmith shop, and a half-dozen houses set at odd angles around them like rocks fallen from a cairn.

"Drag the cable around the east side of the church, Jack, where nobody'll see it. Not that anybody would come around this early in the day.

"The bishop sent Father Rafferty; he was just a tall, awkward, flaxen-haired boy. He used to send the communion wine crashing to the floor in Ned Brannigan's parlor – that's where the first church services were held in the Onamata district. The same families built the church; built it two miles east, in a grove of trees right on the Iowa River, where they planned to move the town when the railroad came through. But *that* railroad was just a rumor and the town ended up a mile to the south, and St. Emmerence of Onamata was left out here on the river bank all by its lonesome. I think that's why it's been kept up so good. Been painted every five years for as long as I can remember."

The church is a rich cream color with brown trim. It's small, as churches go, only about 15 by 30. It has only one door, and there are six windows, evenly spaced, three to each side. Each window is solid stained glass. Mrs. Baron opens the door, which is unlocked, and we walk inside. The church smells of varnished wood and incense.

"Each of them windows was donated by a family in the church," Mrs. Baron says. "We could have had one of them if we'd wanted, but we chose to donate the new organ instead."

The door is at the back of the church. There are rows of pews to seat about 30 people, a small altar at the front, and in the corner at the rear of the church, just to the right of the door, sits an organ. It's not as big as a piano, made of blond wood, and it has a shiny bronze plaque on the face of it. It looks like it's about 20 years old.

She runs her gnarled hands over the plaque. "I could do what I want to do now," she says. "But I don't want you to be a part of it. No use giving us both a bad name."

We climb back in the truck and head for the farm. "'Feels like rats,'" she says suddenly. "John said that to me after the operation, holding his big, square hand against his chest. 'Rats inside me, nibbling away, making me hollow.'"

"It must be very painful for you," I say.

"It's easing pain that's hard. John eased his own pain, shortened his life, by what, two or three weeks? And I don't blame him for it. But the church is so unforgiving. You'd think they were the telephone company or some government department the way they follow rules. A lifetime of faithful service John gave them. For 40 years, before the church was raised up and the partial basement and the furnace were installed, John used to get up at five o'clock every Sunday. When the roads were blown closed, he'd be bundled up in a mackinaw, high up on the seat of his tractor, or before that he used the team, hitched up the cutter, the horses lunging against the drifts.

"But there wasn't a morning when that church wasn't warm when the priest got there, and by the time the congregation started arriving, the old heater would be glowing pink as a piglet and the church so warm people had to take off their winter coats. After the service, there'd be puddles of melted snow under the pews."

As I stop the truck in the farm yard she says to me, "Will you go down to the pasture and catch the horses for me, Jack? I'll try and harness them myself, but I may need some help with that, too."

Two horses graze in a pasture below the house. Barney and Babe are black and shiny as telephones, and they're at least as old as Mrs. Baron, if their age was in human years. They have white patches on their necks where collars have rubbed, and there are soft edges of white along their jaws and around their tired-looking eyes.

Mrs. Baron insists that she can harness the horses alone. "It's not like the truck; they can't take away my license to drive horses." As she struggles with the harness, she talks on.

"The last time I saw John alive he said to me, 'You go on to town, Mary Me Lyle,' using the special name he invented for me when we were courting. He was the last person in the world who used my first name. 'I've kissed Missy and give her a dollar to spend in town. Now I'm going to walk to the pasture,' and from behind the big green chair in the parlor he took out his shotgun. It had green and red flying pheasants on the stock. 'Too many crows about, I'll try to do in a few,' he said. I felt all hollowed out inside, as if his cancer was eating at me, too. His eyes were sunk deep in his face and I could see the pain there, bubbling up in his eyes, no matter how hard he tried to hide it.

"'If I'm not here when you get home, don't you come looking for me – phone the Timneys down the way, Stan and his boys will come by,' and he put one hand on my arm and leaned in and kissed my cheek, the sharp white stubble around his mouth prickling like nettles.

"I watched him walk off, swinging his left leg awkwardly, as he always did. And then I looked over and could see Missy bouncing like a child on the seat of the pickup. I went out and got her and we walked to the highway where Ann Timney picked us up on her way to town."

Now, I watch Mrs. Baron and Missy walk off to the road and make their way along the ditch, which is full of red and white clover, toward the churchyard a mile away, the harness of the horses jingling like fairy bells. When they disappear into the grove of trees that marks the churchyard I get in the truck and drive slowly after them. I want to be close by if she needs help. I park the truck and approach from the back, walking along the banks of the Iowa River. It drifts silently, the color and smoothness of Chinese silk.

Missy is in the churchyard, petting the velvet noses of the old horses, making sweet, bird-like sounds they seem to understand. I peer in the door, and see Mrs. Baron busy winding the cable around the organ, encircling it twice. The ends curl angrily around her ankles as if they have life of their own. She drags one end out the door. She sees me.

"This is my business, Jack. Between me and the church. I don't need no help."

"I won't help or hinder you. I'll just be here if you need me."

The other end of the cable is more of a problem. The last six inches are like a long bolt with a steel circle at the end of it. She taps that circle against the corner of the nearest stained glass window.

I lean against the door jamb. "This window was donated by the Channings," she says. "Last of them is long dead and buried. I remember old Mrs. Channing liked to wear large, flat, blue hats, big as buggy wheels."

The window design is a crucifixion scene, the reds rooster-comb bright, the greens like you might find behind the bar in an Irish saloon. A semi-circular piece of amber glass cracks and drops from the window, making a swishing sound as it lands in the tall grass. She pushes the cable through the break, then goes out and drags each end to where the horses stand, heads down, wheezing quietly in the bright July sun. Missy agreeably steps aside, her hands clasped in front of her, head cocked to one side like a curious bird.

Mrs. Baron unfastens each single-tree, slips an end of cable over each wooden pole, and carefully refastens them. She clucks to the horses, and they plod a few steps until the cable becomes taut. There they stop, unsure, waiting for further instruction.

I stand very still. Thimble-sized bumble-bees drone anxiously over the clover and bluebells. Mrs. Baron waits for a long time, idly holding the reins. An ant scurries over one canvas shoe, climbs the reinforced brown stocking covering her skinny leg, quickly, like a native scaling a palm tree.

Mrs. Baron walks back to the interior of the church, where the cable is already chafing the delicate, thoroughbred-thin legs of the organ. She stares at the brass plaque, and reads the inscription, "Donated by Mr. and Mrs. John Baron," followed by the date. As she stands beside the organ in the cool, peaceful silence, I know she must be considering giving up. It would be so easy. Her voice is harsh from the dark of the church.

"I've already taken some revenge. Last night, I came down here with a trowel and sliced into the mossy earth, around there." She has moved to the door, and points with her small hand to where the graveyard rests on the far side of the church. "I didn't use his gravesite, just in case they check. You never know about those young priests. But I buried him inside the fence. There were tiger-lilies delicate as orange kittens looking down on my hands. I pushed the urn down wrist deep. Yes, them over there. What they don't know won't hurt them one bit.

"I was almost ready to quit there a minute ago. But no, I'm going to give them something to think about – sheep and shepherds alike."

She makes her way out into the light and urges the old horses forward until I hear the cracking of the organ legs, like bones breaking. When the cable becomes taut, the horses stop, back up a step. Then, at Mrs. Baron's urging, they move forward again, and boards groan and nails move in wood, screaming like injured animals. The window-frame cracks, and pieces of stained glass rain onto the wild grasses, allowing pure light to rush in where it has long been denied.

LIEBERMAN
IN LOVE

As soon as he entered the airport terminal, a beautiful Hawaiian girl appeared and slipped a lei of waxen orchids over the head of Lieberman, age 52, a land developer from Denver, Colorado, a widower for almost two years, lonely unto death. As he accepted the lei, Lieberman bent his long form to allow the girl to kiss him on the cheek, all the time thinking that Honolulu had to be one of the loneliest cities in the world.

Across the whole island of Oahu brightly-dressed tourists fluttered like flags in a breeze. But, thought Lieberman, flags are lonely objects, bright though they may be, always separated from their contemporaries, each snapping briskly in the wind, each alone. Alliances formed in Hawaii were of necessity short, often both harried and hurried. Women who lived in the islands permanently did not want to be bothered with tourists; other tourists were, like Lieberman, desperate for contact of any kind. But there were always planes to catch; one-week tours were ending. You could only stand to visit the Polynesian Cultural Center or take a moonlight cruise so many times, he thought.

Lieberman was a good-looking man with a full head of iron-gray hair. He golfed, swam and jogged regularly; he traveled sufficiently to keep a dark summer tan all year round. His trimmed beard and deepset eyes were black and contrasted sharply with his almost white hair. Lieberman fancied that he looked like a magician.

His life since his wife's death had been miserable. She had always worked beside him, was as responsible for their financial success as he was. He had lost not only his lover of 25 years, but his best friend and business partner. His sons, both of whom worked in the business – actually they had made all the major decisions since his wife died – appeared to have written him off, acted as if he had suddenly become untrustworthy, seemed to expect him to join their mother in death momentarily.

After observing an appropriate period of mourning, Lieberman had not lacked for female company. But what he longed for was to be in love. His friends' wives introduced him to their friends; he found himself being asked out to dinner three and four times a week. But his dates were usually wilted women with squeezed, bitter faces and thin hands – women who drank too much and spent most of the evening maligning, rightly or wrongly, the husbands who had abandoned them to the world. Or else they were widows who spent the entire night extolling the virtues of their dead spouse. These types usually had a large studio portrait of the deceased beside their bed. More than once while making love, Lieberman looked up to catch the eye of the corpse. "Oy, Harry never did *that*," one of them might say. Or, "I wish you had known Harry, you could have taught him a few tricks."

He occasionally dated one of the younger women who worked for his company or one that he met at one of the several private clubs he belonged to, but younger women, at least these upwardly-mobile ones, wanted to go dancing, or skiing, or wanted to eat in restaurants that didn't serve real food, but supposedly-healthful concoctions at 20 dollars a plate that looked like algae and tasted like bicycle tires. Lieberman wanted an intelligent, attractive younger woman who liked steak and candle-light, quiet music and sex.

He got so tired of the chase, of boring evenings rehashing his life story for the 20th time in a month, that he settled for satisfying his sexual needs with prostitutes, both in Denver and when he was traveling. In Honolulu, after a number of failures, he discontinued contact with any of the numerous escort services, which took up a whole small section in the Yellow Pages. He liked to walk the Kalakaua strip, breathing the soft, late-evening air, and make his choice from the many young women who discreetly and not so discreetly offered their services. Lieberman often talked to several women before selecting one, negotiating a price, then hailing a taxi to take them to his hotel.

His experiences with the escort services were that they seemed to send whatever girl happened to be available, paying no attention to the height, weight, or coloring he had specifically requested. He had a number of unpleasant experiences – women appeared at his door, who, though young and attractive, were not sexually appealing to him. He had particular difficulty with a tall, toothsome Filipino girl, who was insulted even after Lieberman paid her full fee and tipped her handsomely.

"I earn my money, okay?" she said several times, leaning against the inside of his hotel room door. "Why you no like me? I'm clean. See doctor alla time. You no have to look at me. Lie down, think about girlfriend. I do you good, okay?"

Another time a combative Samoan woman made serious threats against his person after he declined her services, though he paid her in full.

On other occasions he made love to women who displeased him in some minor way. They were too thin, or had scratchy voices, or had shaved their pubic hair, something he particularly disliked.

It took him two weeks to make what he considered a suitable contact. He spotted her standing on the sidewalk in front of a Mrs. Field's Cookie Shop, on Kaiulani Street. She was staring boldly at passersby, nibbling a chocolate-fudge cookie, wearing a knee-length brown leather skirt, a white haltertop, and white high heels; she was blue-eyed with reddish-blond hair expertly styled. She has a mind of her own, Lieberman thought, and she radiates sexuality.

"Hi," said Lieberman, stopping directly in front of her.

The girl, Shaleen, eyed him up and down, licked cookie crumbs from her lips, said nothing.

"So how's business?" asked Lieberman .

"How do you know I'm not somebody's expensive wife who just walked around the corner from her suite at the Hyatt to buy a cookie and take in some night air?"

"That's exactly who I assumed you were," said Lieberman, bowing slightly. "I also assumed you were a woman looking for excitement."

"And you're a man looking for excitement?"

Lieberman nodded.

"Do you have any idea how I hate being cutesy like this?" said Shaleen.

Lieberman smiled. "So do I," he said.

"The kind of excitement you have in mind, with the kind of woman you have in mind, costs," said Shaleen.

"It costs what it costs," said Lieberman .

"We can get a cab at the Princess Kaiulani. We'll go to your hotel," said Shaleen.

Shaleen was what Lieberman was looking for, an accomplished lover, an intelligent companion, a woman with both common and business sense.

Early in their acquaintance, as soon as Shaleen decided that she would allow Lieberman to become a steady customer, Shaleen set down guidelines.

"I don't think you're the type to get all foolish over a working girl, but let's get a few things straight just in case. First of all, I don't have a heart of gold. I'm a businesswoman. I'm not a lesbian and I was never sexually abused. I come from a perfectly normal, middle-class family. I do what I do for the money, and for the excitement.

"You know what I did after my first month on the street? I flew to Switzerland and opened myself a bank account – pretty smart for an 18-year-old, wouldn't you say? I've sent a little envelope of cash off in the mail every few days ever since. I'm 27 years old, Lieberman, I don't do drugs, I don't have an old man, I don't drink myself senseless like most chicks in this business. Most whores give away their money because they feel guilty about how they earned it, well not me. I don't feel guilty and I bet I'm worth more than you were at 27, maybe even more than you are now."

"You probably are. I have something called taxes that bleed me white. Perhaps you should be paying me."

"I'm gonna retire on my 30th birthday. Maybe I'll just live off interest, or maybe I'll buy a hotel, or maybe I'll go into land development. Need a partner?" said Shaleen, laughing.

During his third week in Honolulu, more out of boredom than anything else, Lieberman decided to rent an apartment instead of living out the winter in a hotel. He chose a rental office within walking distance of his hotel. It was the moment that he was introduced to the rental agent that he fell in love.

How could anyone *not* love a face like that? he thought. That she was special to Lieberman only, he knew to be true, but who else was he shopping for? Her name was Kate McSomething. He didn't assimilate her last name, but he could tell from her drawl that she was from either Texas or Oklahoma. She was redheaded with green eyes and freckles, and the twang in her speech made Lieberman's knees weak.

Lieberman had trouble keeping his agitation under control. He asked her numerous unnecessary questions, discovered by looking at her left hand that she was married, was able to establish through questioning that her husband was an officer at nearby Fort DeRussy.

In spite of the fact that the young woman was very busy, Lieberman tried to make the interview last forever. He was disappointed that she could not take him around Waikiki to view apartments; her job kept her at her desk. She was wearing a white peasant blouse that exposed her tanned and freckled shoulders. While Lieberman questioned and salivated, Kate got on the phone and set up appointments with apartment owners or tenants, or set aside a number of keys to vacant units. Her phones were ringing constantly, making it difficult for Lieberman to pry personal information from her. He accepted the keys and a paper with his list of appointments. He loved her large, looping handwriting. He held the paper to his nose when he reached the street hoping some brief scent of her had remained behind. He wanted to rent all her available apartment units, leaving her free to deal only with him. Over the next two days he viewed nearly every apartment her firm had available. When an appointment had been made, he felt he had to keep it, and did. He would report back to Kate after each one. If she just gave him keys he often did not view the apartment at all, simply going to a nearby restaurant for coffee until sufficient time had passed that he could return the key and stare at the face of his loved one again.

On the second day he waited for over an hour outside the office, but out of view from the window, planning to intercept her when she emerged to go to lunch. But she did not emerge. Finally he went back in and returned the last key he had been given. The remains of a sandwich and salad tray were in her wastebasket, a can of Diet 7-Up on the edge of her desk.

On the third day he invited her to lunch. She refused.

"I work right through," she said. "That way I can go home a half hour earlier."

The next day Lieberman tried a new tack.

"I've taken up so much of your time," he said, smiling with as much charm as he could muster, "I'd like to repay you." He waved off her objection and continued. "Tomorrow I'll make reservations for lunch," and he named a revolving restaurant at the top of a 45-storey building.

Kate smiled and Lieberman could feel his heart melt with desire.

"I'll have to dress up," Kate said. "Usually, since I don't go out of the office, I just wear jeans."

Lieberman shaved twice, changed his shirt three times in preparation for the date. Kate wore a white dress with a single palm frond patterned near her right shoulder, and matching green shoes. As they walked among the tourists on Kalakaua Avenue, Lieberman was ecstatic. He made pointless conversation, tried to conjure up ways of making contact with Kate. He managed to guide her by the arm across a couple of streets, into and out of the elevator at the restaurant. As his fingers touched her, he tried to will her to thrill to the contact the same way he did. The lunch was pleasant, but Kate didn't give him any hint of being infatuated with him. He told her his life story, heavy on the widowhood and loneliness, short on his age, the fact that he had a son nearly as old as she, long on his financial success, without appearing ostentatious.

He found out a little about her. She *was* from Oklahoma, had been in Hawaii for a year; her husband's name was Larry, and he was stationed at Fort DeRussy.

Lieberman was cautious not to make any sexual overtures that might frighten her away. He would take his time. He watched her eating a sliced papaya for dessert. The succulent yellow fruit disappearing into her mouth made Lieberman faint with desire.

"I'd be honored if we could do this again, soon," Lieberman said, when he returned her to her office.

"There's no reason," the girl said, staring at him frankly.

"To make an old man happy," he said. "I hadn't realized how lonely I've been," he said. "Friendship only," he added quickly. "You're so young, and married. I'm not making a pass."

"I enjoyed myself, too," she said. "I don't see why not then, in a couple of days. While I think of it, I've got a new listing you may want to look at."

The next week, Lieberman rented an apartment from her, a beautiful, furnished one-bedroom in Discovery Bay Tower, on Ala Moana Boulevard, with an unobstructed view of both the ocean and Diamond Head.

"I'd invite you to my housewarming," he said to Kate, "you and your husband, except I don't know anyone else here in Honolulu; that would be kind of a small crowd."

Kate smiled at him. She wrinkled her nose when she smiled. Lieberman thought he would die of happiness each time she did that.

"I don't suppose," he went on quickly, "that you'd be able to have dinner with me? Just a friendly celebration, you understand. Is there an evening you'd be free?"

To his surprise Kate allowed as her husband bowled in a league Thursday evenings. Lieberman hired a limousine, picked her up at the apartment on Date Street where she lived, took her to Nick's Fish Market, probably the most exciting restaurant in Honolulu, the place where visiting celebrities visited or were entertained. Cheryl Tiegs was there, as was film critic Gene Siskel. Kate had hoped to see Sylvester Stallone, or Bette Midler, both of whom were in the islands, and had been sighted at Nick's on previous evenings.

"It must be wonderful to live this way all the time," Kate sighed.

"Only when you have someone you love to share it with," said Lieberman, fearing for an instant that he had said too much.

But Kate smiled sweetly and said, "You really should be looking around, not wasting your time with someone like me."

"If I don't have a sweetheart, at least I have a friend," said Lieberman, forcing a cheerful smile.

At Nick's, Lieberman danced with her for the first time, held her in his arms, smelled her hair, explored the contours of her body, running his hand up and down her back as they danced. Lieberman was in heaven. He controlled his desires carefully. At the end of the evening, when he walked her to her door, he took both of her hands in his, leaned in and kissed her cheek. She didn't mind. In fact she stood on tiptoes and kissed him on the mouth, a non-sexual kiss of thanks.

Lieberman floated back to the limousine. When he got home he called Shaleen's answering service and left a message. She arrived at his apartment a little after midnight.

"This is my busy time, Lieberman. It's gonna cost you."

He handed her a signed check. "Fill in the blanks," he said. "It costs what it costs."

Lieberman, wanting to know everything about Kate and her husband, called in a private detective. His name was Mr. Woo. He looked like a busboy, Lieberman thought. He reminded himself that the detective came highly recommended by a reputable lawyer. Mr. Woo wore a cheap Panama hat, a cheap Hawaiian shirt, baggy black trousers and sandals. He was about five feet tall, and so thin he might have recently escaped from a country with a food shortage.

Lieberman explained what he wanted to know.

"Involves surveillance," said Mr. Woo. "Time is expensive."

"It costs what it costs," said Lieberman. "Money I've got, information I don't."

He gave Mr. Woo their names, Larry and Kate McInally, their address, the name of the rental agency she worked for and his rank at Fort DeRussy.

"They must never know. You must be certain that anyone you talk to won't report back to them."

Woo bowed slightly, opened his mouth as if to speak.

"I know," said Lieberman, "expensive." He took out his checkbook. "As I'm sure you know, everyone has a price for silence. Neither this man nor his wife must ever know they've been investigated."

Woo smiled as he folded the check and placed it in his shirt pocket.

Six days later the report was delivered by messenger. After reading it, Lieberman felt he probably knew more about Larry McInally than Kate did.

He had lunch with Kate as usual; he explained his excess energy, his edginess, by saying he was waiting for a phone call to confirm a very important business deal. He was so tempted to let slip some of the information he knew about Larry, even some of the things he had found out about Kate that he didn't know. Lieberman felt full to overflowing with terrible secrets.

"I've never seen you like this before," said Kate, laughing.

"Business can be very stimulating," said Lieberman. "A little like hunting, the excitement of the chase, the thrill of closing in for the kill."

He had to wait until mid-afternoon to get through to Shaleen; she left her phone unplugged until she was ready to start her day.

They had finished making love. Shaleen was sitting up, three pillows behind her, smoking a cigarette; her short blond hair was only slightly dishevelled.

"How long are you planning on staying?" she had asked Lieberman earlier, almost as soon as he had arrived. Shaleen's condo was in Yacht Harbor Towers, only a block from where Lieberman rented. Worth $300,000 if it's worth a dime, thought Lieberman.

"All night, if it's okay," he replied.

"It'll cost," said Shaleen.

Lieberman tossed his wallet on the coffee table in front of the velvet chair he was sitting in.

"Help yourself. It costs what it costs," he said.

"Never trust a whore, Lieberman. You'll get burned."

"You just don't want me to know you're honest. Tell me the amount, I'll count it out myself."

She did, and he did.

"For an old guy, you're a great fuck," Shaleen said now, exhaling smoke.

"You're not bad yourself, for a hooker," said Lieberman.

Lieberman and Shaleen were spending three or four nights a week together at either his place or hers. From the day it began he told her about his courting of Kate McInally.

"Still not making any progress with your lady love?" asked Shaleen. Lieberman had come to Shaleen's after his third Thursday evening dinner date with Kate.

Lieberman sighed. "Three lunches a week, dinner every Thursday. What else can I do?"

"Offer her money. Shit, Lieberman, some of these little sex-ratories are just dying to turn an extra buck, especially if their husbands are in low-paying jobs like the military. Offer her a thousand dollars to go to bed with you."

"What if she accepts? I'd have to pay her a thousand each time. It would be the same as what we do."

"It costs what it costs," said Shaleen mockingly. "You pay me. You get a good lay. It would be the *same*. Except you're soft at the center, Lieberman. You're in love. You have the mistaken idea that one woman is different from another. It's alright. My business would drop 80% if men realized women are essentially all the same."

"That's ridiculous," shouted Lieberman. "There's love and there's sex, and there's mutual respect and companionship and caring."

"Sure," said Shaleen. "So how are you gonna get into her pants?"

"I don't know. She loves her husband."

"Kill him," said Shaleen. "Or have him killed. Out of sight out of mind, you know the old saying."

"I couldn't."

"Hell, Lieberman, I *know* people. For $25,000 I could arrange to get anybody knocked off."

"That means if I paid you $25,000, you'd only spend $10,000. Is life that cheap?"

"Cheaper. You underestimate my greed, Lieberman. I'd only spend $2,500. For that price the guy would leave a terrible mess and probably his fingerprints, but he'd never know who hired him or why."

"I couldn't," Lieberman repeated. "He's an innocent man. Probably a decent one. From what she says, he loves her too."

"You're all heart, Lieberman. Why don't you fall in love with me? I'll fall in love with you. Just dig out your fucking check book, write down the number five and keep adding zeros; I'll peek over your shoulder and let you know when I'm in love."

"Wait," said Lieberman. "Maybe there is something you could do. What would make it the easiest for me to win Kate over? If Larry wasn't in love with her, right? If *he* dumped *her*, why I could be the dear, patient, long-suffering friend there to comfort her in her time of need. She'd slowly come to love me."

"Oh, God," said Shaleen, "get me a violin."

"Ridicule from someone who would think nothing of having a man killed, does not move me," said Lieberman. "The problem is *how* to get Larry to dump his wife. And what more logical way than for him to fall in love with another woman?" He smiled at Shaleen. "And that's where you come in."

"If you thought offering her a thousand a trick was expensive..."

"It costs what it costs," said Lieberman. "Money is not the object. I'm in love."

"How nice," said Shaleen. "So, how do you want me to handle the situation?"

"Remember the report I ordered from the detective? I'll get it for you. It's full of photographs. It details his every move, gives the complete history of his life. It tells everything but the length of his peter."

"I'll check it out and let you know," said Shaleen. "Maybe there's a reason why she likes him. Maybe he's well hung. Now, do I tell him I'm a hooker?"

"What do you think?"

"I'll play it by ear. Some guys would be real excited to think a hooker has fallen in love with them, that they're getting free what everybody else has to pay for. Then again, some guys would be mortally offended to find out the sweet girl they think they're in love with, is available to anybody with the money. By the end of the first evening I'll know which kind he is."

"It will be easier than stealing sand off Waikiki," said Shaleen. She had stopped by Lieberman's condominium after her first evening with Larry McInally. "He's a nice, pleasant, boring kid from Creede, Colorado, who went to college on an ROTC scholarship, married a cheerleader, and thinks he's a great lover."

"Is he?"

"Are you kidding? He's 28 years old, was probably laid three times in his life in the back of someone's car at a drive-in movie, before he married what's-her-name? He equates being a good lover to banging me all the way through the mattress to the floor. If he was mine, I'd give him his own fucking manhole cover to play with so he could leave me alone. He thinks pussy is made out of steel."

"You're seeing him again?"

"Of course. When do you want me to move him in with me, tomorrow or the next day?"

"A couple of weeks at least, but keep him overnight next time. I want Kate to know she has a problem."

"I can't imagine it, Lieberman, you're in love with a fucking cheerleader."

The next time they met for lunch, Kate was distracted. No matter what Lieberman said, he couldn't make her laugh. She picked at her food. What made it worse for Lieberman was that he knew exactly what was wrong: Larry McInally had spent the two previous nights with Shaleen.

"It really hurts me to see her suffer," Lieberman told Shaleen over the phone, late that afternoon. "What if I break them up and then Kate doesn't fall in love with me? I don't think I could live with that."

"Developing a conscience, are we? What do you want me to do, feel sorry for you, Lieberman? By the way, dear little Larry is thrilled to death about my being a hooker. He's already planning to get out of the service as soon as his hitch is up; while I will continue to earn my living on my back. I think he sees himself in a ruffled shirt, wearing mirrored sunglasses and spending my trick money on stretch limousines and cocaine. He wonders why I burst out laughing for no reason while we're getting it on."

"Don't frighten him off," said Lieberman.

"You know I don't think I've ever frightened a trick off. I know at least 30 other ways to make a john come, but never by fright."

"Just remember how much I'm paying you," said Lieberman. "That should help you to control your laughter."

"I wouldn't ask you for help if I wasn't desperate," Kate said at lunch a few days later. She was wearing the white dress with the green palm frond, the one Lieberman found so attractive. She reached across the table and took Lieberman's hands in hers. "I don't know what else to do, where else to turn," she went on, her voice breaking. Her eyes were red from crying, her cheeks blotchy. Lieberman had never loved her more.

"I know you like me...maybe more..." Kate said.

"Much more," said Lieberman.

"That's why what I'm going to ask you is so awful. If you say no, I'll understand."

"Try me," said Lieberman.

"I followed him," Kate said. "I hired a taxi and followed him to her building. I asked the security guard what unit he went to, and he told me. That was at five o'clock last night. I waited outside for seven hours. At midnight I decided he wasn't going to be leaving, so I got the phone number from the security guard. She has a silent listing. I phoned, but all I got was her answering service. So I rang the apartment on the intercom, and when she answered I told her who I was and asked her to send Larry home so I could talk to her. The security man let me sit in his office until Larry left. Then I went upstairs.

"I can never compete with her," Kate cried. "She's beautiful and rich and one of her dresses is worth more than everything I own. She was very nice to me. Her name is Shaleen Berger. She owns her own investment business. Larry's madly in love with her. He's planning on moving in with her next week. And she's going to let him. But she's not as crazy for him as he is for her. She hinted around, intimated that if I had some money, or if I had a rich friend who would help me out, that she could be bought off."

Kate held tightly to Lieberman's hands. Her green eyes had a wildness in them.

"I don't have any money. I thought maybe you could loan me enough to pay her off. I really love him. I don't care if that sounds dumb. I just do. I'd pay you back," she rushed on. "And – I'll do anything for you. You know what I mean. I'll go back to your place with you right now, if you'll promise to help me. I know how cruel this must seem, but if you love me, will you talk to Shaleen? Will you pay her what she wants to stay away from Larry?"

"I'll do whatever I can to help you out," Lieberman said. "And you won't owe me a thing. I appreciate your offer, but I'd never take advantage of such a situation. I only hope Larry knows what a lucky young man he is."

Though he didn't need to, Lieberman copied down Shaleen's name, address, and phone number.

"Why didn't you tell me?" Lieberman screamed into the phone.

"I wanted it to be a surprise," said Shaleen coyly. "I didn't want to spoil your fun. I thought you'd be in bed with her, instead of spoiling my afternoon."

"You've ruined everything," roared Lieberman. "I'm coming over, now!"

"You do that, it sounds as if you need somebody to talk to. Whores are always good listeners."

On the way to her apartment, Lieberman considered ways of killing Shaleen. No hired killer for her. He visualized killing her himself, strangling her slowly, shooting her, using a knife. He discarded the methods one by one. He was not, and never had been, a violent man. Was that true? he wondered. He remembered a time years before, when his business was new. Union thugs had demanded a hefty percentage of his profits from a highrise he was building in return for keeping the site free of labor strife. He arranged to meet them at the construction site. As their car drove up, he'd dropped a concrete block from the fifth floor of the skeletal building. He could still see the glass of the windshield rising like water into the midnight air.

"I don't know why you're so upset," Shaleen said, after Lieberman rumbled into her apartment. "If there's anybody who knows I can be bought, it should be you."

"Why didn't you send her away? Why didn't you tell her you were taking her husband, like it or not? It would have sent her straight into my arms."

"But she was so nice," said Shaleen. "The sacrifices some people are willing to make for love, just got the better of me. If she'd come in with her claws out, screeching, I'd have been hard as nails, but she was just so sweet. She could see she was outclassed. I wanted to give her some hope. I suggested she *might* have a rich friend she could turn to for help. It was just a thought. How was I to know? I'd never seen her before," and she smiled at Lieberman, pursing her lips in an exaggerated manner.

"How much are you supposedly asking to send her husband

back to her?''

Shaleen named a figure that caused Lieberman's eyebrows to involuntarily lift nearly half an inch.

"There's a condo two floors up that's for sale for just that amount. I need a little security for my old age," said Shaleen.

"You don't think I'm actually going to pay you. You were working for me. You've already double-crossed me."

"Think how good it'll feel to help young love triumph, Lieberman. Besides, you wouldn't want me to tell poor little Kate that you paid me to seduce her husband. Your little cheerleader is going to get misty-eyed every time she thinks of you for the next 40 years; she'll tell her grandchildren the story of how this wonderful man loved her so much he paid off the evil woman who was taking her husband away from her. You're too much of a romantic to pass up a chance to make the noble gesture of the century."

Lieberman, trapped like an insect on flypaper, wrote Shaleen the check.

"You'll be sorry," he said hollowly as he passed it to her.

"Told you never to trust a whore," said Shaleen.

He met Kate for lunch the next day.

"It's all arranged," he told her.

"I know," said Kate. "She broke off with Larry last night. He came crawling home begging for forgiveness."

"And you forgave him?"

Kate smiled sadly.

"I'll pay you back," she whispered. "I'm flying home to Oklahoma City for a few weeks, kind of to get my head together, you know. Then I'll start paying you back. And the other still applies."

Lieberman declined graciously. A tear oozed out of one of Kate's green eyes and sat on her cheek like a jewel. Lieberman kissed her goodbye, his heart breaking. He wondered what Shaleen had told her. Kate seemed to think there was only a few thousand dollars involved. He was tempted to tell her the truth; she knew the value of a condo on one of the top floors of Yacht Harbor Towers. But Lieberman was too much of a gentleman. He wished Kate well and assured her she need not pay back the money.

Lieberman felt very old in the mornings. He did not open the blinds. He thought of flying back to Denver. He again turned to an escort service for company. The results were most unsatisfactory.

It was during the third week of his mourning that Shaleen phoned.

"I'm coming over," she said.

"I didn't call you," said Lieberman. "What you cost I can't afford."

"Tonight is free," said Shaleen. "I owe you that much."

"And perhaps an invitation to your housewarming?" said Lieberman.

Shaleen arrived all in white, the tips of her golden hair, frosted; several thousand dollars in gold chains circled her neck and wrists.

"I saved you a lot of grief," said Shaleen.

"Did I ask to be saved?" glowered Lieberman.

"You didn't want to be married to a cheerleader. Incidentally, I didn't buy the condo. I used the money to pay Kate off."

"For what?" said Lieberman.

"To go home to the mainland and forget about you."

"Me?"

"Aw, Lieberman, somebody had to look after your best interests. Your cheerleader might not be an intellectual, but everything you did was so obvious you might as well have carried flashcards. Actually it wasn't Kate who came to see me, it was me who went to see her."

"Why?"

"Look, Larry McInally is a jerk. She was delighted to get rid of him. You could have had her anytime from the second lunch on, but you were just too backward to see it. She decided, since there was so much at stake, to play things your way, not frighten you off."

"Then she really cared for me."

"She thought she did. But, as we've both always said, Lieberman, everybody has their price."

"You really paid her off?"

Shaleen nodded.

"You paid her off with *my* money!"

"I'm only willing to go so far. What do you want from me, Lieberman, a declaration of love?"

"How much of my money did you give her? How much did you pocket?"

"Does it make a difference?"

"It would be interesting to know how much I'm worth to you."

"Fraid not," said Shaleen. A working girl's got to have some secrets."

"I suppose you think I'm not in love with her, that I was never in love with her," Lieberman said. It was almost a cry.

"That's what I think," said Shaleen.

"I suppose you think I'm in love with you," wailed Lieberman.

"That's what I think," said Shaleen.

Lieberman sighed.

"We deserve each other, Lieberman. We're both interested in ourselves first. We're ambitious, and we don't give a fuck for ethics. You don't have any business messing around with sad little cheerleaders from Oklahoma City. You'll thank me for what I did, again and again, as the years go by. But tell me, Lieberman, what happens when two people who care mainly for themselves get together? One of them is going to have the upper hand."

"I know," said Lieberman.

"I wonder if you do? Remember, Lieberman, I don't have a heart of gold. I'm interested in gold."

"I understand," said Lieberman.

"I'll spend your money. There'll be a premarital agreement. What's yours is mine, what's mine's my own."

"I understand."

"I'll keep my trick book. There'll be other lovers...whoever and whenever I say. I only have to go to Denver once a year, in the summer, and for no more than 14 days. There'll be times when I'll embarrass you, Lieberman. I'll dress like a whore when I meet your relatives. You'll look like a foolish old man..."

"I understand."

"I'll sleep with your sons."

Lieberman crossed the room, reached out his hand to Shaleen, pulled her to her feet and into his arms.

"I've been widowed once," he said into her golden hair. "It could happen again."

Shaleen laughed into his shoulder. Lieberman thrilled to the sound.

DRIVING
PATTERNS

Hilda and Wesley, driving. Hilda behind the wheel, envies the truckers she sees on the road. She envies them their freedom, their powerful vehicles. She gives the car some gas, and the Chrysler, towing an *Odysseus* camper, glides into the passing lane and sweeps past an 18-wheeler. Hilda glances up at the driver; he has a red, beefy face, with sideburns the red-gold of desert sand. If I was alone, Hilda thinks, I'd get myself a CB radio, though I don't know how I'd learn to tune in the truckers' channels. She thinks on that for a while, decides she would go to a radio store, appear helpless, say she was buying the unit as a surprise for her husband who trucked all the way from Iowa to Georgia and back. Yes, that's what she'd do. See how that hand played.

For a while she fantasized about the golden-haired trucker. Hilda and Wesley are an hour out of Cheyenne, heading toward Billings, and eventually for Banff National Park and the Rocky Mountains. Hilda's professionally lightened hair is the color of a canary. Her body, sturdy as a sack of corn, is covered in a Caribbean-blue, Fortrel pantsuit. She wishes she was young enough to be attractive to the truck driver. She wishes she was not 52. She wishes she was alone in the car. Such thoughts make her feel guilty. She looks over at Wesley, who is sitting against the far door, a white T-shirt covering his pigeon chest. Wesley is reading from a paperback book, his voice a soothing monotone. He is wearing a pair of lemon-colored slacks, brown loafers, and has a self-satisfied expression on his bland face. Hilda wants to do something to shake Wesley up. She lets the car wander over the center line, keeping one eye on Wesley as she does so. He waits a long time before he says anything, but he raises himself higher on his seat, his head closer to the windshield. Hilda is pleased to see that there is genuine fear on his face.

"What are you do..." he starts, but at the first sound of his voice Hilda guides the car back to the proper lane, the oncoming traffic still not dangerously close.

"Don't get all excited," Hilda says, as if she is admonishing a child. Her features are calm, but inwardly she is smiling. This is the third time in three days she has scared Wesley. "Why don't you keep on reading to me?" she says conversationally. Wesley reaches toward the dash and picks up the novel he set down when she let the car wander. The novel tells a story of a senator who is trying to overthrow the President.

Until they retired, Hilda had scarcely driven in her life, although she had always had access to a car, and occasionally drove her daughter, Lorraine, to school, or into Postville to 4-H, Girl Scouts, or something like that. When she and Wesley started traveling, Hilda suddenly discovered that she felt in control behind the wheel of the car. She quickly grew to like the feeling.

Hilda had been raised in McGregor, Iowa, a dying town on the Mississippi River, near the Wisconsin border. After high school, she had gone to Chicago and taken a job with a large insurance company. She sat all day in an artificially-lighted room with 40 other young women, typing case histories. She lived alone in a tiny basement suite in a nice residential district. She put up lemon-drop curtains, and painted and polished and decorated.

"When you meet a nice boy, your apartment will let him know right off that you're a homemaker," her mother had told her.

As they drive, Hilda tunes out Wesley's reading voice. Hilda thinks again of the truck driver, decides that she has had only one truly exciting day in her entire life: June 6, 1952.

She was already engaged to Wesley, in fact he was driving to Chicago to be with her that weekend. On her way home from work, she got off the bus at her regular stop, but as she approached a small grocery store she noticed a magnificent candy-apple-red motorcycle angle parked at the curb. When she was a few feet from the cycle its owner appeared. He was a tall young man with shaggy blond hair, a fierce face with wide-set eyes, and a large, sensual mouth. Hilda had actually broken stride to stare at the young man as he casually mounted the motorcycle. As she continued down the street she turned not once, but several times, to stare at him. She heard the bike roar to life, and as she turned once more, the cycle cruised into the curb beside her. The owner smiled and signalled her to climb on behind him. He was dressed all in denim, the back of his jacket was covered in red and black designs and lettering. Almost in a trance, Hilda complied. The bike idled for a moment.

"Put your arms around me and hang on," the driver said.

Again Hilda did as she was told. She pressed her face against the back of his jacket which smelled of fresh air, grease, and something spicy. He took her about a mile away to where he lived in a junky old house with orange dogs sleeping on the porch.

They scarcely exchanged a word as they made love all evening in his cluttered room. Hilda had a number of sexual experiences that evening which were completely new to her, experiences which were not even mentioned covertly in A Teenager's Guide to Love and Marriage, which she had received as a Christmas gift the year she turned 17. The young man took control so easily. Hilda envied him his ease and expertise. She and Wesley considered themselves daring for making love on the weekends he drove to Chicago. But what they did was sudden and awkward, inhibited by clothes and contraceptives.

In the days following the interlude with the boy on the motorcycle, Hilda was both thrilled and horrified by what she had done. In bed with the biker she had been positively acrobatic; she was sore in a number of places for several days. Hilda was sorry that she had no truly close girlfriends in whom to confide her wickedness. When she called her mother she joked about being sore, blaming it on rearranging furniture. Alone, she fantasized permanent injury, infection, disease, pregnancy. All the old wives tales she had ever heard festered in her head. She checked herself several times a day for vaginal discharge.

That weekend, as soon as Wesley arrived they made frantic love between the crisp sheets of her single bed with its rose-colored satin spread. Afterwards, Wesley was jocular and self-satisfied, thinking he had been responsible for her passion.

Hilda had seen the cyclist on one other occasion, but he had not seen her. As she was walking downtown, a few months later, she noticed him pull up across the street, parking in front of a rather sleazy bar called The Logjam. Behind him, on the candy-appled bike, rode a slim young woman with curly, black hair. The woman was dressed in denim and wore motorcycle boots.

Hilda looked down at herself, at the polkadot print dress she wore, and the white platform shoes with the yellow-daisy fasteners. She tried to picture herself in denim and boots, walking into the rancid-smelling bar on the biker's arm. But she could not.

At first they took turns driving 50 miles each. Whoever finished up at night did not start in the morning. The first summer they even kept a little log book showing how far they traveled each day and who drove each portion of the journey. When Wesley was at the wheel, Hilda secretly hoped that he would drive on and on.

When she knew it was nearly her turn to drive, Hilda would start a new chapter in whatever book they were reading aloud. The freeways were worrisome; the other drivers went too fast; it seemed to Hilda that truckers liked to ride on her bumper.

But, gradually, she gained confidence. The air-conditioned Chrysler padded softly as a cat down the highways. She ceased to be surprised and nervous when she sighted the camper in the side-view mirror. She became expert at backing in and out of parking spaces. Sometimes she forgot entirely about the driving and let her mind wander away from Wesley's voice, away from the car, and back years and years to her one moment of what might have been.

It was through her mother that she met Wesley. She came home for a weekend her first October in Chicago, and went to church with her parents. They attended Trinity Episcopal, and were, like most Episcopalians, rather casual about their religion. Wesley was a nephew of someone in the congregation, an earnest young man in a sport jacket that fitted poorly.

During all their married years Hilda and Wesley never attended church. Once, early in the marriage, when she had suggested it, Wesley replied: "I only went to church so I could meet a good girl."

Wesley was red-complexioned with a sloping forehead and chin, and eyebrows the color of corn silk. He farmed with his father on two sections of prime land near Postville, a few miles west of McGregor. His parents were preparing to retire, and the deal was struck that Wesley would farm the land, split the income with them during their lifetimes, and inherit the land after they were gone. Anything the parents saved from their half would go to Wesley's sister, who was five years older and married to a bank manager in Cedar Falls.

Hilda and Wesley had one daughter, Lorraine, who was agreeable and obedient, and who was in her final year of law school at Drake University in Des Moines when Wesley decided to retire.

Lorraine was now graduated and working for the Peace Corps.

Wesley announced his retirement on his 50th birthday.

"I want to travel," he said. "I want to see the United States."

The announcement caught Hilda by surprise. I'm not old enough to retire, she thought. Won't everyone consider us old, if we're retired? She equated retirement with death. Her few friends told her how lucky she was, most of their husbands were workaholics, they said.

The first summer on the road, Hilda saw more parks, cairns, and museums than she dreamed existed. Wesley began keeping a diary, listing meticulously, like an accountant, all the places they visited. We're drifting across the surface of the United States, Hilda thought. We're like those long-legged insects that glide over placid water, walking so lightly they don't disturb the surface.

The farm had brought an exorbitant price. They were financially secure. After traveling until October, they returned to Postville, where they rented a one-bedroom apartment with a fireplace, which was equipped with glass doors, where they burned colored logs as they spent the winter days watching a super-sized television.

It was during the second summer on the road that their driving patterns began to change. When she was the driver, Hilda began locking her door. She had heard on *Donahue* that most drivers who were injured in accidents were thrown from the vehicle on impact.

Hilda tried to imagine what it would be like to be dead. I haven't even begun to live, she thought. My life hasn't started. It's as if I've lived in a cocoon all these years. Most people consider us lucky and rich in everything. We've had no tragedies, no failures. But there's been no happiness. No real successes. We've drifted. Having nothing happen to you isn't necessarily living.

"What are we going to do?" Hilda asked Wesley, as they floated along the California coast highway in the Big Sur, high above the foggy ocean with its dark rocks, and cavorting seals.

"About what?"

"About us," she replied.

"I thought we were happy," said Wesley.

"I didn't say I wasn't," said Hilda. "What I said was, 'What are we going to do?' Are we going to spend the rest of our lives skimming along highways in the summer and hibernating in the winter?"

"If you're unhappy, we can do anything you want to do. What would you like to do?"

But Hilda couldn't think of anything she wanted to do, except go back to 1952 and start all over again.

"I feel like driving a hundred miles," Hilda announced one day during the second summer. Wesley looked up from the book he was reading. Hilda listened sporadically to the books Wesley read; he listened intently when she read aloud, often asking her to repeat a passage or scene. Wesley bought the books; always adventure novels, political thrillers, mysteries. The one they were currently reading was about a US President who sells out to the Russians, and the Dallas newspaper reporter who was the only person in the world who could stop the sellout.

Hilda drove 150 miles. Wesley drove 50. Hilda then drove for the rest of the day.

In San Francisco she went to a book store and bought several hardcover works of fiction, after asking the advice of the wise-looking book store owner. "Challenging," was the word he used to describe her choices.

But as Wesley droned on from a new book, Hilda's mind continued to float away; she could not follow the stories, there was too much rumination, navel-gazing, Wesley called it. And too much obscenity. It embarrassed Wesley to read sexually explicit passages.

Maybe if I pretend I've been *that girl*, Hilda thinks. Where would I be now? You don't see couples over 30 riding around on motorcycles. Do those men die young? Or do they just get worn down by life like everybody else, and end up as watchmen or janitors, living in two-bedroom rented apartments in small towns. What became of that girl with the black, curly hair, sitting so jauntily on the motorcycle, smoking a cigarette? What becomes of young women like that? Where do they go? Do they become those gaunt women with ravaged faces who sit in taverns, make-up slurred, voices quarrelsome?

Living without passion is the worst thing a person can let happen to themselves, Hilda thinks. She eyes Wesley, who reads on, half smiling.

In April, when they started their third year on the road, Hilda began fastening her seatbelt. She also began doing all the driving. She took the first turn in the morning, and, when they stopped for coffee after about a hundred miles, she would say cheerfully: "I enjoy driving. I'll keep on if you don't mind."

For the first few days Wesley continued to offer to take his turn.

"But I don't mind driving," Hilda would say. "It makes me feel useful. Besides, you read so much better than I do." Wesley would acquiesce, smiling his self-satisfied smile, hauling the current novel up from the floor on his side of the car.

Besides feeling that she has somehow missed out entirely on life, Hilda feels that as she has grown older she has become solider, not just physically, but more visible. She has gained substance, she thinks, while Wesley has lost substance, has faded like one of the black velvet cushions that used to sit on their sofa on the farm. The sun faded the black velvet to the color of dust, the bright oranges and reds of the punchwork flowers, to a uniform cream color. Hilda remembers working Saturdays during high school at an old-fashioned Woolworth's, with dark counters, the whole store smelling of baking donuts. Remembering the store, she realizes that she has come to think of Wesley as one of those pale, translucent fish that used to sit languidly in the greeny aquarium water at Woolworth's. The boy on the motorcycle she thinks of as one of the plump, black fish with protruding eyes, aggressive, full of danger.

At an entrance ramp to I-15, near Great Falls, Montana, Hilda pulls into traffic too soon and too slowly. On her bumper, a trucker sounds his foghorn-like horn.

"Watch out!" cries Wesley.

"Don't be so grouchy," Hilda yells at the truck as it growls around them. "If I had a CB, I'd give that fellow a good earful."

"You were at fault," says Wesley.

"He was speeding," says Hilda sullenly.

She makes herself comfortable behind the wheel of the Chrysler, pats her lemon-colored hair, checks the rearview. It will be a long day.

"I sure wouldn't mind hearing a chapter of that book," she says, making her voice cheery, congenial.

They spend the night in a quiet, mom and pop motel and trailer park near the Canadian border. Over breakfast Hilda maps out their route, using a vermilion-colored felt marker to widen the road until it looks like a river of blood on the map.

Wesley begins reading as soon as they are gliding along the interstate. He bought a western novel in Billings, and an evil land baron is bringing in a hired hand gunslinger to keep the homesteaders in line.

Hilda has a vent open so the wind blows full onto her face. She steers the car with her fingertips, wheeling it into the passing lane and zooming around a semitrailer. She breathes deeply, experiencing the wind in her face, the power of the cycle between her thighs, the muffler snarling as she feeds gas to the engine. The boy from long ago sits behind her now, his strong arms clenched securely around her. She presses the accelerator. Beside her, as if obscured by the blur of speed and blue-tinted glass, Wesley drones on, sunning himself. Hilda increases speed, the roar of the cycle fills her ears. She envisions winding mountain roads.

Eyes fastened on the book, staring neither right nor left, placid and self-satisfied, Wesley turns himself slightly in Hilda's direction, adjusting his posture in the death seat.

ELVIS BOUND

We drove up Highway 26 from Charleston and picked up Interstate 40 near Asheville, North Carolina. We'll visit Tyler's grandmother in Knoxville, then spend a few days at the Grand Ole' Opry before heading on to Memphis. This is our first genuine family holiday in the middle of summer, up until now I've been playing for or managing a baseball team all the years I've been married.

The kids are in the back seat of our brand new stationwagon; they're pounding around and singing "We are marching to Memhem-fuss, as we have done before," though none of them have ever been to Memphis.

A visit to Graceland, Elvis' homestead, is going to be the highlight of the trip for everyone but me. Somehow I've had enough of Elvis, and it don't matter how excited Tyler and the kids get, I'm not about to be impressed. I couldn't be impressed now if I wanted to; I've made too much fun of everything about Elvis. It's even got to be kind of fun, them lined up on one side and me on the other.

"I hear they have three of Elvis' pubic hairs in a golden dish with a crystal dome over top of it," I say to Tyler. "They've got an old Egyptian attendant with a turban on his head, who, for an extra dollar, will let you look at them hairs just a laying there like curly cracks in the golden plate."

"Oh, Dad," says our oldest girl who's 14, easily shocked, and would, as she says, "expire from embarrassment," if she knew even part of the story I'm about to tell.

"What's a pubic hair?" says Austin, our youngest, who's named after the city in Texas, 'cause that's where I was managin' the year he was born. You think I didn't have a fight on my hands over that name? Tyler, she was hell-bound on namin' the boy Elvis.

Tyler finally gave in, not because she backed down one inch, but because she'd had her way when it came to naming the girls. The oldest's Priscilla, and then Lisa Marie is 10. Lisa Marie is just dyin' to see the airplane with her name on it that they rolled up on the lawn across the street from Elvis' mansion.

I sneak a look over at Tyler and it's hard for me to realize that she's lived almost half her life as my wife. Nobody gave our marriage the chance of a snowball in hell. Consequently we didn't get interfered with much. The only person who caused us grief was Elvis Presley. Elvis damn near broke up our marriage until I found his weakness and got the best of him.

Tyler was 16 and waitin' tables in a Sambo's in Baton Rouge when I met her. We were married within a month, against everybody's advice – my folks, my manager, my friends on the team, and Tyler's probation officer. She'd been a sort of juvenile delinquent; never raised, just dragged up by a mama who o.d.'d on something when Tyler was 10. She'd spent time in foster homes and orphanages, lived on the street for a year, was workin' her second shift on graveyard hours at Sambo's when I met her. Tyler never held what her mama did against her. I remember maybe the second night we were together cuddled up in the front seat of my car in the darkest corner of Sambo's parking lot, waiting for her to go on duty at midnight when I said something about how awful her childhood must have been. She snuggled into my neck and said, "It was just that Mama never met a soft-hearted ballplayer." And I guess it was at that moment I knew I loved her, and that ain't ever changed, or ever will, in spite of what Elvis tried to do to us.

"I did everything but turn tricks," Tyler told me early on, "though a couple of guys I lived with at times sure wanted me to. I don't know why I didn't. Some of my best friends on the street were whores. I guess it was just that they never seemed to have a pot to piss in or a window to throw it out of, in spite of all the tricks they turned. All that money just passed through their hands..."

Tyler had her initials tattooed on the back of her left hand, T.P., for Tyler Presley. And she has another tattoo, a little blue rose just below her left collarbone. I been lovin' Tyler for almost 15 years now, and I still get hard as a baseball bat when I see that little tattoo. If it wasn't on there good I'd have licked it off years ago.

Tyler is dark skinned with lazy blue eyes that never seem to get all the way open. She looks like there are little weights forcing her lids down. She's got small, even teeth, and crow-colored hair that glints with greens and purples in some light.

Let me explain about that name Presley. It's not that she's a relative...well?

Ty-lah was the way she pronounced her name when I met her. Her voice lost some of its softness over the years as we've kicked around from Baltimore, to Indianapolis, to Oakland, to Cincinnati, to Syracuse during my 13-year, undistinguished career, up and down from Triple A to the Big Show a dozen times with half a dozen teams, as a utility infielder. I spent three years managin' in the minors, then a former teammate who happened to make six or seven million dollars during his career offered to take me into his business. We bought a nice home in Charleston and I look out for his interests in South Carolina and Georgia.

So my baseball career paid off in the long run. Some of my teammates called me Hoover, because of the way I vacuumed up ground balls. But the sad truth was I never could hit the curve, and the last couple of seasons I couldn't hit the fastball either. Then this new breed of shortstop came along, guys like Ozzie Smith, Alfredo Griffin, Spike Owen; they cover more ground than I ever dreamed of. So I became dispensable and got outrighted. I managed. I got invited into business. This is my summer to really get to know my kids.

I've noticed, just in the few months since we settled permanently in Charleston, that Tyler's speech has softened again – she's a chameleon, able to adapt. Her voice hardened, became clipped and curt the summer we were in Boston, in Omaha a nasal twang crept into her voice.

Tyler was born in '57 at the height of the Elvis craze. Her mama was a 16-year-old rock and roll groupie. Her family name was Clowers, but she named the baby girl she bore nine months after an Elvis Presley concert in New Orleans, Tyler Presley.

Tyler lived some of the time with her grandmother, some of the time in foster homes; she spent part of her childhood bein' dragged around the country by her mother, who, to put it kindly, never got her life together. Not that Elvis Presley was to blame for what happened to her; if it hadn't been him it would have been somebody else. The way I see it, a certain percentage of teenage girls are destined to be rock groupies or baseball Sadies. The glitter of the costumes, the thrill of the uniforms, the aura cast by men in the public eye, draws these girls in.

"Trouble is," Tyler said to me once, "men in the public glare are electric – like bug lights – their victims are zapped and left for dead.

The only picture Tyler has of her mother is one taken a year before she died. She was one of those women who must have been very beautiful as a girl, but who aged rapidly. In the photo she has sunken cheeks and suspicious eyes, a coyote leanness brought on by years of too much whiskey and too little sleep.

"'I knew it wasn't him. I know fantasy from reality,' Mama said to me just a week before she killed herself. 'But tellin' that story gave me somethin' nice to think about all those months I was expectin' you. He, your daddy, was a boy in a leather jacket, with a nose that had been broken. I'd stayed around after the concert until the hall was empty and the doors were locked and there was nothin' but me and blowing newspapers in the parking lot. I hitched a ride. He was drivin' a 1953 Chev Bel-Air with blue terrycloth seat covers. He had a pack of Winstons laying on the dash and a pair of foam rubber dice dangling below the mirror. I helped myself to a cigarette the minute I got into the car. I slid right over beside him. The car radio was on loud to a rock and roll station and Elvis was singing "Don't Be Cruel." That's all I know about your daddy, Hon. I was hitchhiking a ride after the Elvis concert. He stopped for me. I never gave him a chance.'"

In the back of the stationwagon our kids are singing again, and our sheepdog, Col. Tom is barking.

"Y'all settle down," says Tyler. But she and I smile at each other, and that glance says – as long as the sounds are happy and don't break our eardrums – everything's okay.

Priscilla fancies herself a songwriter. And, putting a daddy's pride aside, she may well be. She plays the guitar and puts on concerts for us. She begins to plunk away. Tyler turns down the volume on the tape-deck where Elvis was crooning "In the Ghetto."

> I just dropped by to see
> If you would talk with me

Prissy has a mournful country twang in her voice. "A good front porch picker and singer," is how Tyler describes her.

> I was too wild to see
> There was no tellin' me
> Now, there's no tellin' you

A creditable lyric. Prissy sings her own compositions at school talent shows.

"She must have inherited her talent from her granddaddy," whispers Tyler, as she bares her teeth in what I know is both a secret and a sexy smile.

This Elvis business, whatever the truth of it may be, has been the plague of our life together. Elvis Presley was like a religion to Tyler's mama. She followed him around the country, sometimes dragging Tyler with her. Once a lawyer fellow got to talkin' to Tyler's mama and he wanted to start an action on her behalf, an action to make sure Elvis acknowledged his child and provided for them both. He said he wouldn't need to take nothin' to court but photographs of Tyler and maybe Tyler herself. He said Tyler looked more like Elvis than Elvis. But Tyler's mama wouldn't hear of it. "I'd never want to cause Him a moment's grief," is what she claimed she said to the lawyer. In those days Tyler still believed Elvis was her father, was some kind of god that was one day gonna come down off the stage or screen and sweep her and her mama up and carry them off.

"I grew up believin' in Santa Claus, the Easter Bunny, the Tooth Fairy, and Elvis Presley."

Like children who are indoctrinated early and often in the mythologies of religion, and who grow up feeling guilt and unease when they come to realize religion is no more substantial than, say, the Tooth Fairy, so Tyler, as the child of Elvis' most devoted disciple, was affected. Her obsession with Elvis nearly destroyed our marriage.

I suppose it would have helped if I had been an Elvis fan. But I wasn't; though I did have big, blue-black sideburns when we met. I've just never liked Elvis much. I was raised on old-time country music. I always took it as an insult that the same people who wouldn't touch rock and roll with surgical gloves accepted Elvis just because he was a good ole' Southern boy from Mississippi, and they took that pig-sticking music of his to heart just as if it was country. Being five years older than Tyler and comin' from a family that still played Jimmy Rodgers' blue yodels and train songs, and owned every record Hank Williams ever made, I just didn't get taken in by the Elvis craze, or Chubby Checker, or the Beatles, or whatever came after them.

But when you're in love you don't think too much about what kind of upbringing your sweetheart has had, or what her hangups are. At least I didn't. Tyler wasn't living much of anywhere when I met her, but within three days she was moved into my little apartment. The place was supposed to be furnished, but about all I'd brought with me was a lot of dirty socks and a case of Bud for the refrigerator. I gave Tyler 200 dollars and said, "Do your best to make this little box a home." And she did – with curtains and bright yellow dishes, throw rugs and a Leroy Nieman reproduction of a reproduction of a ballplayer swinging at a bad pitch. And! A life-sized poster of Elvis on the wall right beside our bed, and there was a little pink light covered with a frilly shade. The light turned Elvis' white jacket pinkish, actually seemed to make his sequins glitter, and cast a nasty aura around his head, making it look as if it he were winking.

The first time Tyler reached up her arm and turned on that light was just as I was lickin' my way down her belly; I had discovered that she could be induced to make the damnedest pleasurable noises and I was all set for some enjoyable listening. I damn near died of shock.

"Shhhh, Love," she said. "Ain't that the prettiest thing you ever did see? Between you an' it I'm straight on my way to heaven."

"I don't want that patsy watchin' us," I said, and decided then and there I'd been mistaken about Tyler. Too many hangups, I told myself.

"Oh, Baby," Tyler said, "close your eyes and make me cry the way you did last night."

And I did. She was new to me. She went wild when we made love. I like noisy women. All the time we made love Tyler sobbed and shrieked and carried on like some girls do at a concert.

I brought up the business of Elvis in our bedroom a couple more times, but Tyler just said things like, "It don't do no harm and it makes me as horny every night as if you just came home from a 10-day road trip."

"I think it's sick," I said. "You grew up thinkin' that weirdo was your father."

"But I know he ain't," argued Tyler.

"What if I wanted to drool over a picture of Marilyn Monroe while I was gettin' it on with you? Wouldn't that piss you off?"

"Not if I knew you loved me best. And I do love you," said Tyler.

I'd always let the subject drop, but I seethed inside, and more than once I considered finding me a woman who didn't need to stare at Elvis Presley to get her rocks off. But then Priscilla came along, and when I looked at her wizened up little face, why, I fell in love without even trying.

I mean, what was I supposed to do? There was nobody I could talk to. Young ballplayers aren't supposed to have to worry about anything except their statistics. My manager that summer was one of those guys who had read too many books by Dale Carnegie; he used your name in every sentence of every conversation, and liked to slap his players on the back a lot and deal only in positive emotions. In other words he was a twat. He'd say things like, "That was a hell of a hit you made in the second inning last night, Ben. It was a good pitch and you just overpowered the ball. I really like the way you're swinging, Ben, and the way you contribute to our offence. However, Ben, I think we should talk about the ball you misplayed in the seventh..."

Even though he encouraged communication, actually wanted us to talk over our personal problems with him, I just couldn't imagine myself saying to him, "Skip, my sex life is driving me crazy. My old lady stares at a life-sized poster of Elvis Presley all the time we're fucking."

I got out a sheet of Tyler's notepaper one night, and got as far as writing, Dear Ann Landers, before I tore it up.

It's difficult to compete when your wife is in love with Elvis Presley.

"I wouldn't mind it so much if you got off on John Wayne, Mickey Mantle, James Coburn, somebody with balls," I told her over and over again. "Fucking Elvis couldn't get it up with a block and tackle. He just lies around Graceland with his Memphis Mafia, all good ole' boys, if you notice, and gets fatter. I hear he's gonna be spokesman for Butterball Turkeys. It takes one to know one."

But nothin' I said made any difference to Tyler. That languid poster of Elvis continued to live right beside our bed. Tyler still insisted that the "adoration light" as I called it, remain on while we made love.

I remember once after my team had been on a road trip to Tucson for a five-game series, I was just wild for Tyler when I got back. The team bus dropped me off a block from our apartment. Tyler was curled up on the sofa watching TV when I came in. I just took her hand, pulled her to her feet and marched her right to the bedroom. She hardly had time to put her cigarette out and was still exhaling smoke when we got to the bedroom door. Still, even though I was kissing her like she had diamonds hid in her mouth, she reached behind me and turned on the adoration light as I was laying her down on the bed: Elvis in a white rhinestone jacket and black slacks, reclining on a chaise lounge, looking sleepy and greasy, his lips slightly parted in what might have been the beginning of a sensual smile, or what might have been a sneer of contempt for all the foolish, wet-crotched women who got excited by his pose. Elvis, I thought, probably got it up for cocked revolvers, and seven-foot black basketball players from Uganda.

Tyler undid her blouse and rather than taking it off just tossed it open to show off her round, freckled breasts: to me a few clothes are more erotic than pure nakedness. I undid her jeans and pulled them down. The first time I ever undressed Tyler, in that little apartment in Baton Rouge, when I helped pull her jeans and panties down, I said, "Throw your fucking panties away. If you're gonna be my old lady you don't wear panties." Tyler tossed her panties to the furthest corner of the room. What I said totally surprised me, for I'd only met Tyler a few hours before. Baton Rouge was a sweet place for a young ballplayer that summer, and I'd averaged at least three women a week when we were in town. But I knew Tyler was the one. And she is. Except for a long time there was this Elvis thing.

This Elvis thing. I mean I wouldn't touch the psychology of it with a 10-foot pole. I'm not a scholar. I don't suppose I've ever read a book I wasn't required to. I was raised in Kentucky. My daddy was a foreman at a strip mine. We had a couple of spotted hounds under the back porch, a pickup truck and a pitcher's mound in the back yard. I never could pitch though, and Daddy took to hittin' me grounders in that uneven sloping yard.

"If y'all can field in among them gopher holes and jack-grass plants, it'll be easy for you on a regular field," Daddy said, and he'd spit tobacco juice so it flowed with the wind, and whack me another twister.

I don't suppose I knew any psychology, except what's dished up like butter on grits, on the Sunday Night Movie, until one year when I was with the Oakland A's. We'd lost 15 in a row, and our team batting average during the slump was .188. Charlie O. called in a psychologist to find out what the trouble was with us.

I guess that psychologist was pretty tired by the time he got to me. I was either the 24th or 25th man on the roster. If somebody had to go it was either me or the mop-up reliever, the guy they brought in when the score was 9–1 in the seventh inning. That kind of reliever is known as Whale Shit and he gets left in no matter what kind of trouble he gets into. I was what's called a Puffball, a defensive infielder who couldn't hit his age, let alone his weight.

"Well, Ben, suppose you start by telling me how you feel about your teammates and management," the psychologist said. Another Dale Carnegie groupie. That opened lots of doors. I knew most of the guys were complaining about the food on the road, the way the press wrote about us, the things Charlie O. said about us. Not very exciting stuff.

"Call me Ian," the psychologist said. He was a skinny guy about my age, dressed in an A's jersey and baggy jeans. I figured him for a guy who would trade the remaining years of his sex life to start three games at second base and get one hit off Catfish Hunter. Since Charlie O. was known in baseball circles as Cheap Charlie, I knew this guy wasn't getting paid. He was probably doing it because he got his rocks off by being around professional ballplayers.

"I've got personal problems," I said. Actually I was batting 1 for 3 during the slump and hadn't made any errors in the field. Ian smiled and then looked serious. He was finally going to get some stuff he could sink his teeth into. He'd told a couple of guys that they were trying to get back at their own fathers by annoying Charlie O. And what better way to annoy Charlie O. than by not hitting or fielding or hustling.

"My old lady's in love with Elvis Presley," I said. Then I explained everything about Tyler and Elvis and the adoration light, and how it pissed me off that Elvis was getting credit for all my hard work in bed.

"It's not as if Tyler is empty-headed," I said. "I'd have got shorn of her soon enough if that was the case. She's smart. Smarter'n me, I have to admit." Soon after we were married it became apparent that Tyler knew how to handle money. Over the years she's checked every deal my agent wanted to make. I never brought in big bucks, like some players, but Tyler saw to it that we've always been comfortable; she vetoed some deals, found some of her own even. "A lot of the guys want a stupid wife," I explained to Ian. "I want a wife whose only question is 'Which place you want to put your cock, Sugar? My old lady keeps her mouth shut and her legs spread; the way it ought to be,' are the kind of things my teammates have said to me."

Ian talked for about an hour, so long that the Whale Shit reliever went out for a beer and missed his appointment. He talked about complexes, libido, unconscious and collective unconscious, and somebody named Ed, all of which meant as much to me as stock market quotations. But finally he said something that made sense. "Ben, what would you do if it was the real Elvis Presley there in your bedroom, and not just a paper doll? Would you bust his chops, or what?"

I had to smile at the silliness of it all. I mean there's been an Elvis tape or record playing in our house every waking hour for the past 15 years. When Austin had pneumonia a year ago, was in the hospital and we were afraid he was dying, the only special thing he wanted was to hear "In the Ghetto." Well Prissy plucked on her guitar and we sang it to him, her in her high, sweet, bluegrass voice, me in my hound dog bass that is only occasionally on key. That damn kid was like a wilted flower sponged with water. Hearin' that song did the same for him as a visit from Jerry Falwell might for some of the bonehead Baptist kids in the ward with him.

"I'd be better off if he *was* real," I told the psychologist. "I don't know if I'd bust his chops or not. But I'd be able to do something. Once, right after we were married, I took down the poster while Tyler was out. Tore it up and put it out with the trash. Tyler never said a word to me. She just looked hurt, her bottom lip turned down, and her chin kind of trembled. I guess as soon as I headed for the ballpark she split for the record store. When I got home after the game Tyler was sittin' on the sofa bare as a jay bird from the waist up. Soon as I led her into the bedroom I saw that there was a brand new non-flyspecked poster of Elvis on the wall. What with Tyler touchin' me the way she's so good at, already crooning in her throat as she kissed on me, I didn't have the inclination to complain about Elvis."

"Why don't *you* pretend a little?" Ian said to me. "Pretend it's the real live Elvis Presley dropped into your bedroom to watch. Find out how you'd act."

Elvis was already dead by then. But not for long. His death didn't cause Tyler and the kids as much grief as I would have expected. She did put a black wreath on our doorknob. And her and Prissy sent flowers to Graceland.

"It ain't as if we was close family," she said to me. But I look at her and I wonder. She looks so much like Him. Maybe the only smart thing her mama ever did was to lie about who Tyler's father really was. All she had to do was look in the mirror to see what her obsession had done to her. Maybe she figured Tyler deserved better. "I've got him here in the posters and records and pictures and statues. He ain't ever gonna change. He'll never get any older, and that's even kinda nice. And I can always listen to his records and tapes." I was touched by what she said, by how strong she was. I even stopped bad mouthing Elvis for a month or so.

This will be Tyler's second trip to Graceland. She went down from Austin on a bus tour to celebrate the fifth or sixth anniversary of Elvis' death. She came back laden with geegaws and souvenirs. She brought me a black baseball cap with GRACELAND in fluorescent green letters across the crown. She brought postcards of Graceland viewed from land, sea and air. She bought records from a store called EP's LP's. Prissy still has the bag they came in hangin' on the wall of her room. And there were these really gross photographs of the Meditation Garden where Elvis and all his family is buried. The place is decorated with plastic flowers and there's blue religious crosses, tall as a man, look like they're made of toilet-brush bristles. And there's plastic wreaths bigger than you see at the Kentucky Derby, and little photographs imbedded in the lawn. And they named the street in front of Graceland, Elvis Presley Boulevard. Crass. Gross. Grotesque. But I'm the only one seems to think that way.

That psychologist didn't help the A's win a pennant. The team eventually pulled out of the slump on its own and finished the season with about the record a sub-mediocre team deserved. Ian, the psychologist, didn't help me as a baseball player. I got sent to the minors in mid-August and didn't see the Bigs again until the next spring when I was 25th man on the Minnesota Twins roster. But some of the things he suggested helped me with the Elvis problem.

I wasn't entirely sure what I was gonna do the next time Tyler and I made love, but I had a sneakin' hunch. I kissed down Tyler's belly, licked her inner thighs, parted her lips with my tongue. I moved my tongue in slow, massaging circles, fast as a butterfly, then slow again. Tyler groaned, stiffened her legs as she came the first time, gripping the bed clothes, crooning her love. "Baby, Baby," she cried deep in her throat. Then she actually cried out loud, gasping for breath, sobbing. As always the more passionate she became the noisier she got. As she thrashed beneath my mouth rapidly reaching a second climax, I opened my eyes and stared up over Tyler's belly between the flattened mounds of her breasts. Her mouth was open, her lips swollen with passion. BUT! She had her head turned and was staring at the pink-haloed poster of Elvis. It wasn't me between her thighs that was giving her pleasure. It was fat Elvis in his rhinestone jacket, his oily hair greasing her thighs.

I leapt off the bed so suddenly Tyler screamed and half sat up.

"I got you, you son of a bitch," I yelled. "I knew you been spying on us. But now I got you. I'm gonna show you what we do to fucking voyeurs."

"Y'all gone crazy or what?" said Tyler. She was sitting up, one hand over each tittie, as if I'd really caught someone spying on us.

"That's right. That's exactly what I've gone. I've gone fucking crazy."

I stepped across the room, naked as the day I was born, my shadow crossing Elvis' shadow. I picked up a baseball bat, a favorite of mine that I'd been taping and sanding early in the evening.

"Alright, motherfucker, you're gonna need about three million dollars worth of dental work when I get through with you," I roared.

"Ben!" Tyler cried.

The poster was a new one, made out of some kind of embossed paper – it was almost 3-D, with Elvis' features raised, his sideburns were crinkly, his jacket was silky and the sequins glittered like sandpaper. He was as real as somebody dead can be.

I raised the bat.

"That's right, beg, you motherfucker. If you don't say the right words in the right order, I am gonna be known as the man who killed Elvis Presley with a baseball bat."

"Ben, you're gonna wake the kids," said Tyler in a desperate attempt to distract me.

"That's better," I said to Elvis. "You fuckin' well better be sorry. You better fuckin' apologize for all the grief you've caused me."

"Ben!" Tyler's eyes were wide.

"Alright, I won't kill you," I said, lowering the bat. "But you can't buy me either. No sir. I caught you redhanded, peeping tom, and you're gonna suffer for it."

"Ben?" said Tyler, pulling a sheet up around her neck, her brow furrowed. "You feelin' alright, Ben?"

She started to get out of bed.

"Stay put!" I said. "I'll take care of this sleazy creep."

I got the roll of tape from the chair when I'd been fancying up my bat. I stripped off a piece the length of my arm span, the tape making that stickety-click sound as it unpeeled from the roll. The poster was fixed to the wall by its corners, so I was able to get my hand behind it in the middle. I ran the tape across the back then whipped it across the front so a black bar held Elvis' fat arms pinned to his side. I circled him three more times with the tape.

Then I tied his legs at the ankles the same way.

"I should blindfold the son of a bitch," I said to Tyler. "Hah! Imagine that. He'd have to lie there and listen and sniff the air. He'd look like one of those photographs in the newspaper when they put a black bar across someone's eyes to hide their identity."

"Ben, I think this is crazy."

"Not any crazier than you starin' at this fat-assed freak while we make love. If we're gonna stay together, he stays tied up. He can watch us, and you can watch him. But I'm the one in control. He's trussed up like a turkey goin' to market and he's goin' to stay that way."

And he has.

"What am I gonna tell the girls when they come in here during the day," Tyler said.

"You'll think of somethin'. Tell 'em Grandpa Elvis likes to be tied up."

There's a good chance we conceived Austin that night. Didn't we have a time though. Every once in a while I'd holler over at Elvis, "See what I'm gonna do to her now you sleaze bag."

Elvis has stayed bound all these years. And him being that way keeps us both real happy. He travels with us too. Tonight, after the kids are asleep in their adjoining room at the motel, why we'll unzip Elvis from the full-length suit carrier he rides in, and prop him up somewhere where Tyler can see him good. And I'll say something like, "You reckon our sex life would be any better if some fat-assed ole' rock and roll singer with a greasy curl on his forehead had sneaked in here and was a watchin' us?"

"I suspect it just might perk things up a bit, if you know what I mean. What do you figure you'd do if you caught a fellow like that spying on us?" Tyler grins as sexy and evil a grin as any woman ought to be allowed.

"Why I'd capture him, tie him up and make him watch."

"Would you now?" and Tyler smiles again.

I look down to where she's cuddled up beside me on the car

seat, her nose just a touchin' on my bicep. I love her as much as I ever have or ever will, and 14 years have gone by like an hour.

"We are marching to Meh-hem-fuss," sing the kids. Col. Tom barks.

OH, MARLEY

"'Oh, Marley, you dumb bitch,' he said to me, 'I'm gonna kill you,' and then he took out the knife."

Marley, across the tiny table from me, takes a sip of her coffee. She lights a cigarette, flicks the paper match into an amber-colored ashtray. She is explaining to me why we can't make love, ever.

"He called his knife an Arkansas toothpick, though somebody else told me a real Arkansas toothpick has a long, thin blade – a stiletto, that's it. I knew he carried it; I mean you don't live with somebody for three months and not know he carries a knife in his boot.

"Tod looked real graceful when he drew it out, even though he was out of his head, drunk, and blissed to the gills on every kind of drug you can buy on the street. He had a three or four inch slit up the back cuff of his jeans so he could whip those pants away from his boot and draw the knife all in one motion. He showed me more than once how he could do it, when he wasn't stoned or drunk. In fact he showed me the first night I ever brought him home with me, after I'd met him in a bar called Hanrahan's: him sittin' and grinnin' all lopsided on the little loveseat I had in my apartment – one

I'd made real pretty yellow slipcovers for, yellow with big crimson squiggles. It was kind of scary, but kind of a thrill too, to have a boyfriend who carried a knife."

Marley is new to Vancouver, new to this house, moved in the first of the month to a room across the hall from me. A table, a two-burner black gas stove with white porcelain handles on the jets, a tiny half-fridge the size of a TV, a single bed, a wardrobe; I know what's there without ever being in her room, for all the rooms in this old house are the same. Marley is a big girl-woman. She's 19. Woman or girl? The first time I saw her she was wearing a baby-girl-pink coat, white stockings, white shoes. I thought perhaps she was a nurse.

I first spoke to her at the mailboxes in the front hall. She was wearing faded jeans, a long-sleeved man's workshirt of blue and black plaid. I'd guess Marley weighs close to 300 pounds. I like big women. Some guys do. I don't think about it, though I have a friend who wants to apply Freudian interpretations to everything anyone does. "Back to the womb," he says when I talk about my fondness for big women. Then he rambles on about Jocasta Complexes. I point out that he's gay and I don't try to analyze him.

"Since you're new here maybe I could show you around downtown," I said to Marley in that dark, varnish-smelling front hall. "We could go to a movie, maybe out for a drink afterward. I get pretty lonely up there in my room trying to write all the time."

I had read her name on the tag on her mailbox, lettered on a strip of coffee-colored plastic tape, something the landlady made up each time she got a check from a new tenant. *M. Sconiers*, it read.

"I guess that would be okay," she said about my request for a date. "I'm Marley, short for Marlene. Everybody calls me Marley." Then she said, "You're sure you don't know me?"

"No, I don't know you," I said, puzzled. I decided to treat her statement as a joke. "You must come from the East," I said. "Here in Vancouver we don't let radio or TV waves or even newspapers come in from the East. We have our own world here. It's a great place to start over, or hide out."

Marley just stared at me in the dim hallway. I thought there was genuine fright in her eyes. She had a wide, pale face with a few yellowish freckles on her cheeks and across the bridge of her nose.

"I'll knock on your door at seven. Hey, don't change clothes. I don't like dresses, okay?" My Freudian friend would get a few miles out of that.

"I didn't want to think he was serious," Marley says, drawing on her cigarette. "But I knew he was. His eyes were a faded blue with tiny chips of bright blue trapped in there like sunlight. I mean he didn't have nothin' to be mad about. I never messed around on him, and I cooked. Used to cut recipes out of *Family Circle;* I'd cook him things that was healthful. Of course they didn't always turn out. He was mad because he knew we had a half-bottle of Southern Comfort in the cupboard, but it was gone when he staggered in to look for it.

"'I gave it to Monique,' I told him. 'She was goin' to a party and both her and her old man was broke, so I loaned it to them.' Monique was a good chick; she'd of paid me back.

"'You're holdin' out on me, you bitch,' he said, and he slapped me, openhanded. 'You dumb bitch, I need a fucking drink.' And he slapped me again on the same side of the face. After the first slap I'd sat down on that pretty little loveseat.

"It was just like the time when he owed money to somebody and he wanted to turn me out, you know, make me turn tricks to pay off his debt. 'I'm no whore,' I told him. 'You can slap me all day and I still won't turn no tricks for you.' That time he gave up. Later on Tod said how sorry he was for how my eye looked and all. He got some money someplace and bought me a whole carton of Baskin-Robbins. Then we got it on, and wasn't it good.

"Another time he brought this friend home with him, Derek

was his name. Tod made sure I had four or five drinks, and we smoked a little weed. Then Tod started comin' on real strong, you know he unbuttoned my blouse and started playin' with my tits, and this with Derek sittin' right on the other side of me. I said, 'Hey, we got company,' and Tod just said, 'Oh, Marley, you just be a good girl now and we'll make you feel better than you ever felt before.' I hardly even realized it but they each had a nipple in their mouth, and the tops of their heads was touching. Derek was cute in a kind of dangerous-looking way; he had a full head of black, black hair, all shiny and sleek, like Elvis used to look.

"I shouldn't be tellin' you this, should I? It's just that I been here in Vancouver for over a month and you're the first person even noticed I'm alive. I'm a talker, no question. 'When Marley starts talkin' it's like turning on the bath water full blast and havin' the tap stick on you,' was what Tod used to say. 'You need to run her down with a semitrailer to get her to shut up.'

"The only other person I've talked to since I've been in Vancouver is my doctor. I had to fill out this little card the first time I went to his office, even though I'd been referred to him by my doctor in Hamilton. Hell, he's a psychiatrist. You might as well know. I'm not one to keep secrets. Everything out in the open. That's just my way. They asked me to state on that card what my problem was. You know what I wrote down? *Acute loneliness*. And it just about blew the nurse's mind. She looked at me like I was a real freak or something. I mean that is my problem. They claim if you know your problem you're halfway to a solution. Isn't that true?"

"I'm sure it is," I said, barely getting the words out before Marley plunged on again.

"That's why we can't get it on." She smiled at me. Her eyes were a soft, hazel color.

"Because you're lonely, or because you're seeing a psychiatrist? I don't understand."

As I had suggested, we had gone to a movie, a Woody Allen twin bill; one of the movies starred the girl who played *Mary Hartman, Mary Hartman*. "I like Woody Allen," Marley said, "his characters don't fit in either."

We held hands at the movie; Marley let me kiss her once, but that was it, *let me*. Afterward I brought her to this ice-cream parlor/café, a brightly-lit place. We each ordered a strangely-named dish with lots of whipped cream, chopped almonds, and chocolate sauce. It may have been called a Tar Baby or a Tarred Roof.

I suggested to Marley that I'd like to spend the night with her. I can tell by the way she looks at me now that she wants to. After the movie we walked for a while, arms around waists, past the closed downtown shops, thighs rubbing, giggling like children at the window displays, at our reflections in the neon-pocked windows.

"I can't spend the night with you because of Tod. Because of what he did."

"I don't care about Tod. He's in your past. Remember you came to Vancouver to start over."

"I can't let you see me," she says, a tear oozing out of an eye and sitting like a dewdrop on her pink and white cheek. Marley's hair is a lemon color, the shade 70-year-old women dye their hair. One of the first things she did, it may even have been in the hall of the rooming house, was to assure me it was her natural color. "Nobody has this color on their own. It embarrasses me," she said.

"He used the knife," she goes on, wiping the tear away, drawing in smoke, trying not to cry. "Tod used the knife on me. But the worst part is I lived. It would have been so simple if he'd killed me."

"Oh, Marley," I said, reaching across the glass-topped table to take her dimpled hand. "Tell me only what you want to tell me. People don't have enough time to be curious about the past. I'll tell you a story about me if you like..."

"Not now. I've got to tell you about what he did to me. If I tell you you'll know why I can't show you," and she looked at me miserably. I hadn't realized she was wearing mascara, but the lashes of the eye that had cried left a dozen black dots on her cheek, so neat and well spaced they might have been an unusual beauty mark.

"'Oh, Marley, you dumb bitch,' he said, pulling the Arkansas toothpick out of his boot; then he stabbed me on the right side just below my rib cage. Actually it chipped the rib, the doctors told me at the hospital. I didn't feel anything, a twinge, not what I'd imagined being stabbed would be like.

"I was still sittin' on that cute little loveseat, the one I'd covered in yellow. I couldn't believe it. I stared down; I was wearin' a white T-shirt and jeans. I was barefoot. I remember thinking, Tod don't like me plonking around the apartment in my bare feet, he's told me so a few times, that it gets on his nerves. Maybe if I'd been wearin' shoes, or my boots, these same ones I got on tonight, maybe he wouldn't have stabbed me."

"Marley is wearing a pair of soft suede boots, the right one is badly worn. I've noticed her weight turns it almost on its side each time she takes a step. The waitress brings more coffee. Marley takes a new cigarette from the open pack on the table. I take the book of matches from her hand and light it for her. She smiles.

"I looked down," and she looks down now at the black-on-blue flannel shirt she is wearing, as if expecting a rose of blood to appear on the front of it. "There was a big, tomato-sized splotch of blood and it was growing – all I could think of was wine. And I remembered reading in *Family Circle* about how to take out wine stains. Was it cold water? Salt and water? Vinegar? I thought all those things in the couple of seconds before Tod stabbed me again. He was dancing around like a madman, holdin' the knife like he was swordfightin' or something, stickin' me with it again and again.

"He hit my arms, both of them, and blood just leapt out and splattered on the yellow loveseat cover. He hit my chest. It wasn't like you'd think; the pain wasn't awful. Just a twinge each time, like a growing pain, or a minor cramp. Then one thrust hit my belt, and the next one went in just above it, and the next and the next. He drove the thing into both my thighs, and both my breasts. All I could think of was I was being murdered, and it didn't feel near as bad as I would of expected.''

"Marley, are you telling me this because you want me to understand you, or because you want me to dislike you enough to walk away?''

"I'm tellin' you why we can't ever be anything but friends. I like you, but I can't ever be," and she paused helplessly, not able to find the right word, "*that way* with anybody ever again, no matter how much I want to.''

"Shouldn't I have something to say about that?''

"You don't know the whole story.''

"What I know, Marley, is that people don't hate you because something awful has happened to you, or even because you've failed. People hate you for being a success. They can forgive almost anything but success.''

"I'll never have to worry about that. But maybe what you say is true because what happened to me was an odd kind of success. I became a celebrity, or curiosity would be a better word.'' She paused for a moment. "About the twentieth time Tod stabbed me I started to feel faint. I guess I'd been screamin' all the time, but I don't remember that. They say Tod was yellin' too. I just started to feel dizzy and like I was sinking down into a big, fluffy feather comforter. I remember thinkin', if this is dyin', it ain't scary at all.

"Somebody called the cops. They got there pretty quick. I guess 'cause both of us was screamin' bloody murder.'' She paused. "That could be a joke, couldn't it? Anyway, they ran up the stairs and kicked in the door to our rooms. They say Tod was standin' over me, stabbin' me the way someone real frustrated pounds a pillow. The cops drew their guns and told him to stop, but he didn't even slow down so they blew him away. Each cop put a bullet in him. He never stopped swingin' the knife; as he was fallin' dead he stabbed me in the leg, just below the knee.

"They radioed for an ambulance. They say I was spurtin' blood in dozens of places, like a punctured garden hose.

"The ambulance men hauled me out of the house, me layin' on my back big as a whale on the stretcher. Nothin' might have come of it, I mean publicity and pictures and stuff, if this freelance photographer hadn't been listening to police calls. By the time they hauled me out he was there, his flashbulb popping a mile a minute all the way from the front of the house to the ambulance.

"That photographer not only sold the picture, he sold a story to *National Enquirer*, and the next week just as I'm startin' to feel a little better, there I am on the front page, all ugly and bloody as a side of beef, under the headline:

Woman stabbed 73 times suffers no serious injury!"

There is such a fine line between pathos and humor that I have to bite the inside of my mouth, firmly, to keep from laughing. I have always had the ability to mentally step back from a situation and see it as it really is. On one hand Marley is pathetic: big, and stupid, and pathetic. But on the other hand there is a terrible innocence and vulnerability about her. I do not laugh.

"It was terrible to see that story. It would have been better if Tod had killed me. The picture was taken from the most unpleasant angle, from below as I was being lifted into the ambulance. I looked like I was made of inner tubes. The strain of my weight showed on the faces of the attendants.

"And the story wasn't even serious. It laughed at me. 'Emergency room doctors stated that 57 of the wounds could have been potentially fatal to an ordinary-sized person.' It went on to say that because I weighed over 300 pounds, the knife couldn't get in deep enough to hit any of my vital organs. There were copies of that *National Enquirer* at the nurses' station and in the waiting rooms at the hospital. People from all over the hospital came to look at me. Local TV came. A girl from the TV station phoned me and was real sympathetic, said I'd get a chance to tell my side of the story. And I did. I guess she didn't have anything to do with the editing though. The story came out as a series of shots of this whale in a white gown, with first the TV reporter talkin' and then my tinny little voice in the background. The *National Enquirer* even ran a follow-up story; it called me The Heinz Lady, you know, because of the 57 wounds that might have killed me.

"It was as if I wasn't a person at all. Everyone smirked behind their hands. I was a freak on display and I wasn't even gettin' paid for it like a freak in a circus would.

"I've got 73 scars on my body. I can't even stand to look at myself, so I know nobody else can. Sometimes when I look down at myself, it looks like there's pink worms all over my body, wriggling and wriggling, and I want to run away screaming. But it's something I can't ever run away from. I'm sealed up inside this skin. The one person I want to get away from most I can't."

"Let me tell you a story, Marley," I say. I push my cup to one side, and reaching across the table take both of her hands in both of mine. "Let me tell you a story, because that's what I do. I sit up there in my room – I have a view of the schoolyard across the way where girls in green-and-white jumpers play grass hockey on soft spring afternoons. I tell stories that no one else reads, except editors, who send them back to me. I pretend, Marley. I pretend so hard that I dig my nails into the palms of my hands until I draw blood. I don't even know I'm doing it until it's done.

"I came here to start over too. I've had five years of pretending that it was the right thing to do. Do you think you're the only one with bad memories? Marley, I have a little girl growing up a thousand miles from here. I have a past too. I haven't always lived in a lonely room in a crumbling rooming house. I have scars too. But mine are on the inside, and I'm responsible for most of my own wounds. It seems to me it would be easier if I could blame my scars on somebody else..."

I talk on for another 10 minutes, but with little success. I tell Marley some of the details of how I quit my job as an up-and-coming executive in order to write, and how my wife quit me when I quit the job.

"She's remarried now, to a sales manager for a pharmaceutical company, and my daughter is being raised with all the advantages my wife feels she's entitled to. She'll be a debutante when she turns 18."

I've made my pitch, and Marley seems to have turned it aside. Conversation runs down.

"I guess it's time to go," I say.

"I guess it is," says Marley.

The old-fashioned ice-cream parlor/sandwich shop where we are having coffee also has a bakery counter, but it is closed this late at night. On the way out we pass a refrigerated case where eclairs, cream puffs, jelly donuts, and turnovers sit on wax paper-covered trays waiting for morning. A variety of cakes, some large as trailer tires, doubled and tripled by mirrors, reflect enticingly, their cool, iced surfaces spangled with brilliant yellow and pink rosettes.

As we leave we stop by the display case to admire the repetition of cakes, some with Vs cut from them, revealing their inner composition.

"Don't they look good," says Marley.

"I'll get you one if you like."

"Oh, but they're closed," says Marley, pointing to the dark and deserted counter.

"Everything is for sale if the price is right and the buyer persistent enough," I say.

An old Greek sits at the family table at the back of the shop, nodding over an empty coffee and a full ashtray.

"Hey!" I call, tapping a coin on the top of the glass counter.

"Closed," the old man calls, barely raising his head.

"We want to buy a cake."

"That one!" I say to Marley, pointing. On the bottom shelf at the back is a round, chocolate-iced cake, with a circle of white rosettes, like whitewashed stones around its circumference. Inside the circle, written in white script on the brown background, is the message: *'Best wishes, Sam and Renata.'*

"Why that one?" says Marley.

I clink the coin on the counter again. The old man glares toward us, reluctantly stands up and makes his way across the room.

"Marley, let's pretend," I say. "Let's start over completely. Sam and Renata didn't pick up their cake. So let's take their place. Let's make believe."

"You're crazy," says Marley, but she is smiling as she says it.

"We want that one," I say to the proprietor.

"You the people?"

"Yeah. Renata's plane was delayed," I say.

"Since noon yesterday? I give up on you. Ordered by phone, not even no deposit."

"I've been at the airport, waiting," I say. "I sent my cousin Luigi. My dumb cousin. You must have a dumb cousin," I say to the old man. "He's still out looking for this place. I loaned him my car. We had to take a taxi in from the airport."

"Sam," Marley says, hugging my arm. "I met Luigi once, he's not that dumb. He's not that dumb," she says to the proprietor, but slowly and hesitantly as if speaking a new language for the first time.

The old man laughs. "I got a brother like that; three times we set him up in business, three times kaput," and he spreads his hands in a gesture showing the emptiness of his brother.

He boxes the cake. I have just enough money to pay for it.

"Good luck," he says, and waves as we leave the shop.

It has rained recently. The night is cool and fragrant, the streets blue and deserted.

"So where has Renata been?" Marley asks, again speaking with hesitation.

"You came West for the first time," I say. "Our fathers

arranged the meeting. We both come from solid, old immigrant families. 'You been a bachelor too long, Sammy,' my father said to me. 'I talked on the phone to my old friend Guido in Hamilton last night; he's gonna send his daughter out for a visit. Her name's Renata; you gotta meet her at the airport.' He sounded just like the Godfather when he said it." Marley laughs and snuggles her face against my shoulder. "I didn't want to at first. I mean I don't like my old man messing in my personal life. And I met Guido once when I was a kid. I mean, forgive me, he's your papa and all, but he looked like a gorilla. That's what I was expecting, a little, wizened up gorilla girl. I met the plane out of respect for my papa."

"You're right about how Daddy looks. But he's good-hearted. I was scared to death too. I figured the poor guy who was supposed to meet me would sneak off into the crowd when he saw how big I was. I was afraid he'd know about me...you know..."

"Renata's all over that," I said. "You didn't have to worry. Everything's worked out. If Papa had only told me you were a big girl they couldn't have kept me away from the airport with soldiers. See, maybe we'll hit it off good and maybe we won't, but you're attractive to me, and that's important..." I go to say more; I'm inclined to babble when I'm in a difficult situation.

"Shhhh, Sam," Marley says, "let's just walk for a while."

We make our way slowly toward home, through the dark, lilac-scented streets of East Vancouver. We each have an arm around the other's waist. Marley carries the cake snug in its cardboard box, holding it by its knotted green string.

"Pretend hard, Marley. Pretend hard."

She snuggles her head against my shoulder again. We come to a stop beneath a tall, drooping lilac. Marley raises her face to be kissed. Beside us, where a line of yellow streetlight touches a lilac coil, Tod's knife lurks, glittering, sinister, waiting for one of us to make a mistake.

TRUTH AND
HISTORY

Miss Paskins is one of the only tenants in The Castle, the rambling, multi-additioned rooming house in East Vancouver where I reside, who remembers the previous owner, Wang Ho. Tenants in a rooming house change with depressing regularity, rootless as corks in their lonely bob through life, the rooming house a beach where they rest between tides.

"Wang Ho lived in the glassed-in sunporch at the front of the house, and rented out every available inch of space," Miss Paskins tells me. We are drinking tea in her tiny room that is stuffed with kitten-faced oven mitts, the arms of her sofa and easy chair decorated with tatted and crocheted doilies. China knickknacks are everywhere, gifts from distant sisters and nieces, perhaps former pupils; Miss Paskins is a school teacher who took early retirement because of 'bad nerves,' brought on in part by a disastrous love affair.

"He could have lived comfortably. He was wealthy from owning a large restaurant in Chinatown," she goes on. "Just after World War II ended, when there was such a terrible housing shortage, Wang Ho hired a couple of men, illegals probably, to clean out the hen house in the back yard, where he kept a dozen or so Rhode Island Red hens, and a dozen more stylish-looking white Leghorns. He put all the chickens in a gunnysack, live, and carried them off in the direction of downtown; I guess he served them at his restaurant. The hired help put down floors and installed glass where there had been only chicken wire over the windows. The renovated chicken house was rented out to a soldier from North Carolina and his Canadian wife, who had a squirrel coat, and an awful Russian first name that sounded like Dvorjak. She was a Doukhobor, one of that strange religious sect who burn down each other's houses, and hold naked parades – at least the women do.

"The soldier and his wife had to share a bathroom with the family who rented the room behind the furnace. The chicken house had a wood stove and candles; I guess it was romantic for them, being newlyweds and all. Yes, Wang Ho rented every space that could be rented, and at top dollar. There were no nosy building inspectors in those days.

"After the housing shortage cleared up in the mid-50s, Wang Ho went back to having chickens again. Kept them right up until he died."

The hen house still stands, forlorn and neglected, used now to store garden tools, rusted unrecognizable items that may have fallen off automobiles, appliances, and goods abandoned by tenants who have skulked away in the night leaving ugly objects, unpaid rent and the odors of poverty. The present owner of The Castle, a Mrs. Kryzanowski, is required by law to keep the orphaned possessions for several months before they are trucked to an auction or the city dump.

"Wang Ho was very tall for a Chinese, and he always wore gray, long-sleeved gray sweaters over gray shirts, and baggy gray trousers. I don't know when he ever ate. He kept tea in the sun-porch, but he must have eaten at his restaurant. He was very gentlemanly, always bowed to me when I paid the rent, and he loved to show me the canaries he kept in two, tall, bamboo cages in the sunporch. There were six or eight of them, yellow as dandelions, most of them no bigger than my thumb.

"One evening when I came to pay the rent, Wang Ho looked very sad. He was sitting in an old, overstuffed chair, and there was a stack of purple air-mail letters on the chair's arm. There were orange-colored, foreign-looking stamps in the corner of each envelope and vertical lines of Chinese characters on the fronts.

"'You look like you've had some bad news,' I said to him.

"'Yes,' he replied, cool as you please. 'I have just been informed that my wife is dead.'

"Well, you could have knocked me over with a feather. I didn't know Wang Ho had a wife. He told me then, that he not only had a wife, but a son. He also told me he was 61 years old and had been in Canada for 35 years.

"'Why didn't you bring your family over here?' I asked. I mean he was a businessman, he could have afforded to.

"'Ah,' he sighed, 'the time was never quite appropriate to have my wife join me.'

"It was less than a month later that Wang Ho asked me to marry him," Miss Paskins goes on. She is in her mid-70s, with ermine-white hair and a pink face. Her eyes are a pure, sky blue, and her small nose twitches like a rabbit's when she is excited. Miss Paskins has never married. She dresses immaculately in pinks and blues, stylishly but inexpensively. "I considered the matter for 48 hours and I told him yes." Miss Paskins looks as though she could play an all-American grandmother on a TV series. "That was the biggest mistake I ever made. He always behaved like such a gentleman I thought he could be trusted."

This is not the first time Miss Paskins has told me this story. We have been tea-drinking companions for over three years. Miss Paskins is a basically honest person and she thinks that what she is telling me is both truth and history. Much of her story is neither.

If I am to be honest, it was greed that propelled me to investigate,

in order to establish what I call "The True History of Wang Ho."
In the beginning I didn't doubt Miss Paskins' story, but having, in
the days when I actually held steady employment, several unpleasant
experiences with a branch of government called the Public Trustee,
an agency that looks after, or appropriates would be a better
word, the estates of people who die without any known next of
kin, I decided to investigate to see if Wang Ho's relatives in China
had been cheated out of his estate. If he, indeed, owned a successful
restaurant in Chinatown, then his estate would have been
substantial.

I began by consulting ancient copies of *The Vancouver City
Directory*. Thirty years ago coverage of Chinatown, or even of
houses owned by Chinese was not very accurate. Most directory
personnel were Caucasian, the Chinese were perceived as secre-
tive. Early listings for The Castle described it merely as *Occupied*.
In a later directory the owner's name was shown as Wang, O.
Sometimes his name appeared in the alphabetical section, more
often it did not. While most Caucasian names were followed by
occupation and name of employer, no such listings appeared after
Wang, O. One directory, in what I guessed to be the year before
Wang Ho's death showed simply *R'st'rt* after his name. I was now
forced to spend money.

At the Land Titles office I checked the ownerships of The Castle.
There I discovered something surprising. From 1939 to 1975 The
Castle had been owned by On Ho Wang Low, cafe owner. Going
back to the directories, I discovered a listing one year for a Wang
Low, Prop. Green Garden Restaurant. The Green Garden was
one of the oldest, largest and most successful restaurants in
Chinatown.

"We were engaged for almost two months," Miss Paskins has told
me several times. "We drank tea together in the late evenings. We
agreed vaguely on a spring wedding. At least I suggested spring
and Wang Ho didn't object.

"'I'd like to see your restaurant,' I said to Wang Ho more than once. 'There are certain formalities to be observed, dear lady,' was his reply to me.

"And then came the day when I found out what kind of man he really was. It was a Saturday and a young man came knocking on the door of the rooming house and inquiring about Wang Ho. He was Chinese and was wearing a beautiful blue suit and a cream-colored Panama hat. 'I am from the Department of Immigration,' he said. 'I am inquiring about the gentleman who owns this building,' and he rattled off a long name that had Wang Ho in the middle of it. 'Could you tell me, please, the approximate date of his death?' 'He's as alive as you and me,' I said. 'He went off to work just an hour or so ago.'

"'Ah, there must be a misunderstanding,' the young man said. 'The Department has had inquiries from his wife in China who reports receiving a letter a few months ago reporting her husband's death.'

"'But I thought the wife was dead,' I blurted, obviously more upset than a stranger should have been at hearing such information.

"The young man smiled sadly. 'Not an uncommon practise among immigrants,' he said. 'When they want to, ah, start a new life without any complications.'

"Well, I never spoke to Wang Ho again," Miss Paskins assures me each time she tells the story. "And he never tried to contact me. I guess that man from Immigration talked to him at work. I mailed my rent to him after that, even though we lived in the same building."

As I've intimated, my motives were not solely to see that justice was done. I imagined my liberating the restaurant profits from the Public Trustee; I imagined a grateful family arriving from China to oversee the operation; I imagined them awarding me a 10% interest for my trouble. Even a 5% interest, I decided, would enable a would-be writer, with two suitcases full of unpublished manuscripts under his bed, to write full time and not have to drive taxi, wait tables or teach remedial English. I imagined I might eventually settle for eternal gratitude and free food at the restaurant.

I ventured into the Green Garden about three in the afternoon, the quietest time of day for a restaurant, and asked to see the manager.

"That would be Mr. Tang," a hostess in an aquamarine-colored Chinese-silk dress informed me.

A few moments later a middle-aged man in a business suit appeared, smiling from a round, unlined face. His hair was a neatly combed iron-gray. I carried a large looseleaf binder. I wanted, at first, to be mistaken for a salesman.

"I'm studying the history of East Vancouver," I told Mr. Tang when we were settled in his office, pointing at my notebook. I wonder if you could tell me a little about the original owner of the Green Garden, Mr. On Ho Wang Low?"

"You have done some research already," Mr. Tang said, still smiling. "The gentleman about whom you inquire was known only on legal documents by the name you mention. His true name was Wang Ho, but there was an unfortunate misunderstanding with an obstinate immigration official. All his life in Canada he had to use the other name where legal matters were concerned."

As we talked, I kept revising my estimate of his age upward, from 45, to 55, to 65, to close to 70. I asked Mr. Tang a number of times during our talk if he were related to Wang Ho, but he politely evaded the question, as he did my inquiries about the disposition of Wang Ho's estate, though he assured me that the government had no hand in the running of the business.

I then broached the delicate matter of Wang Ho's engagement to Miss Paskins.

"I suggest you might well have a future as a detective," Mr. Tang said. "The incident you describe is, to the best of my knowledge, known only to the parties involved and myself. I would like to do my best to erase your negative opinion of Wang Ho and to acquaint you with the truth of the situation, but in order to do so I need your word that the information will not be relayed to Miss Paskins."

I promised.

"To put it simply," said Mr. Tang, "what was involved was a misinterpretation of pleasantries. There are, you will agree, in every culture certain phrases exchanged in conversation, polite mouthings which are virtually meaningless?"

I nodded my agreement.

"For instance, when we met in the foyer, I acknowledged you and inquired of your health, and you inquired of mine. Such acknowledgements are always answered in the affirmative, unless one or the other of us are about to meet our ancestors. Even then we usually state our health to be adequate at the particular moment. Do you agree?"

"I do."

"Then you will allow me to explain further," said Tang. "In some oriental households, politeness and custom require that if a guest compliments the host on possession of a certain item, a painting perhaps, or a vase of distinction, the host will bow and say, 'It is yours, my friend.' The guest will in turn bow and say 'You are too kind.' The exchange is meaningless in the context of that society, but a stranger to such customs might assume that the object of his admiration was indeed a gift, and, at the end of the evening attempt to leave with it."

"What would happen if such a mistake were made?"

"Oh, the guest would be allowed to depart, but later on an elder of the community would call, probably with a good translator, and explain, with many apologies, that a mistake had been made."

"Are you saying that Wang Ho's proposal to Miss Paskins was not a proposal but was misinterpreted by her?"

"You are entirely correct."

"But how..?"

"I, though much younger, am from the same village as Wang Ho. There was a custom in our village. I am uncertain whether it was practiced in other villages, for we were isolated and traveled little. But in our village, if you called at the home of a spinster woman, and if you were an eligible male, you complimented that spinster woman on her demeanor and her dress, and added, even if she were very old and you were very young, or vice versa, 'Would you do me the honor of becoming my wife?'

"The spinster woman would acknowledge the proposal by saying 'You are too kind. I shall eventually let you know of my decision.' And the conversation would carry on. You see, everyone in our village also understood the rituals of courtship, so such a proposal of politeness could never be misinterpreted as the real thing."

"Then it must have come as a terrifying surprise to Wang Ho when Miss Paskins accepted his proposal and announced their engagement."

"An understatement. And, you must realize, Wang Ho had no network of family and elders to fall back on. He confided in me because I was from the same village."

"But why didn't he go to her himself, explain what had happened?"

"The logical thing to do, of course. But Wang Ho could not stand to lose face in such a manner. There is an ancient saying 'It is better to be thought a rogue than a fool.'"

"Then Wang Ho's wife really was dead?"

"That is true. Otherwise he would never have made the polite proposal."

"And the man from Immigration? I recall Miss Paskins' recitals that Wang Ho only denied bringing his wife to Canada; the son was never mentioned. Perhaps you once owned a brilliant blue suit and a Panama hat?"

"You give me too much credit," said Mr. Tang, smiling, making no denials. "Perhaps the man in the Panama hat acted out of love, or gratitude, or perhaps the fine clothes were his reward for playing a role."

"Thank you," I said. "It is always a pleasure to learn the truth."

" A truth perhaps," said Mr. Tang. "No one ever knows *the* truth. If you consider carefully, I have had almost 30 years to prepare a defence for Wang Ho. Is my story any more plausible than that of Miss Paskins? There is another ancient saying 'History is determined by the one who lives to tell the story last.' In which case, I wish you a long and prosperous life."

EVANGELINE'S MOTHER

"Henry, I'm putting her on the first flight in the morning," Rosalie said in her rapid, slightly shrill voice. "She's impossible. Absolutely impossible. Alex and I can't do a thing with her."

Rosalie went on to list and elaborate on all of Carin's faults. She cut school. She was probably doing drugs. Her friends were undesirables. She had been arrested for shoplifting a bottle of nail polish, and Rosalie had had to take a day off to accompany her to juvenile court. She was disrespectful, lazy, and promiscuous.

Henry was surprised that Rosalie even knew the word *promiscuous*. "She's fucking around," is what he would have expected from Rosalie.

"She'll arrive at 10:00 A.M. Can you meet her?"

"Of course I'll meet her. And don't worry, I know how to handle Carin."

Henry Vold was slightly below average height, his straight blond hair was professionally styled around a square, reddish face. His eyes were pale blue, his lashes and eyebrows so blond as to appear nonexistent. He had recently grown a small, precisely-trimmed mustache that had to be viewed from the side to be recognizable as anything but a shadow.

Rosalie kept him on the phone for over an hour, enumerating Carin's shortcomings. He found himself smiling, only half listening. He had, he realized, been waiting 15 years for this call, ever since Rosalie had walked out on him and had taken their baby girl with her.

Henry met Rosalie the year after he graduated from high school. A friend arranged a blind date. Rosalie was a tough, flat-chested little blond, with a straight blue-eyed stare, and a chip on her shoulder. They were barely settled in the back seat of the friend's car at the drive-in theater before Rosalie had her hand in his pants. When he fumbled too much, she helped him undo her belt and unbutton her jeans. He probably got her pregnant that night, or on one of the next 14 consecutive nights when they made love in the back of the friend's car.

After high school Henry had taken a junior position with a savings and loan company. He burned with ambition and planned to work his way up very quickly. His own father was a glass installer, a quiet, colorless man, living from paycheck to paycheck in a small, rented house. Henry wanted more for himself, a lot more.

He babbled to Rosalie about his plans for the future. He didn't notice that she paid no attention, that to Rosalie the future involved only who was having a party on the weekend. Rosalie's mother was dead, and her father had been left with "a litter of pups," as he called his children, in his gruff, good-natured way. He was a bricklayer, who, though he drank too much, was a friendly drunk. He worked a few months in the summer, drew unemployment in the winter.

Though neither of them really knew it at the time, Rosalie wanted a man just like her father, unambitious and good-hearted, someone who was at home a lot. Instead, she got Henry Vold, a young man who took the responsibility of a wife and family very seriously indeed.

"Listen, I didn't expect you to marry her," the friend who arranged the blind date said. "I just thought you needed to get laid."

Henry actually asked Rosalie's father for permission to get married.

"I save one-third of my salary. I've already got investments," Henry told him. Rosalie's father, who had never even had a bank account let alone an investment, looked blankly at this serious, formally-dressed boy, and suggested that Henry move in with them.

"Hell, one more won't make any difference. Two, I expect. I don't know who the hell'd want to marry Rosy if she wasn't knocked up." He laughed and slapped Henry on the back. "We'll just have to put the twins to sleep in the attic and you two can have the other room. You'll have a whole parcel of built-in babysitters..."

Henry was horrified. He rented an apartment for he and Rosalie, in a quiet building not far from where he worked.

Rosalie left him just after Carin's first birthday, the week after he'd been made assistant manager at the savings and loan. She took only her clothes and a few of Carin's clothes and toys. She left with a boy who drove a custom-painted red roadster, and worked at the corner service station. He had a braying laugh and bad teeth. *They* moved in with Rosalie's family.

Henry accepted her decision. But he remained a dutiful father, spending time with Carin every week while he still lived in Cincinnati, and seeing her in the summers and at Christmas, after his firm moved him into management and transferred him, first to Cleveland, then to Albuquerque.

He waited five years before he married again, this time to a financial analyst with a firm of stockbrokers, a cool young woman who wore lipstick, smelled of expensive perfume, and understood the importance of upward mobility and planning for the future.

Now, at 36, he had a 16-year old daughter who was being

parachuted into his life. He was not disappointed. He adored Carin. He and Mona had a planned child, an eight-year-old boy named Vaughan, Mona's maiden name. Vaughan was a serious, unobtrusive child, and Henry loved him, but when he thought of Carin his heart positively swelled. He knew his blood ties to Carin were the strongest of all. He could see himself in her. She was having a very difficult adolescence. In Carin he could see what he might have become if he had lacked self-discipline. She had his brains and her mother's fierce, spit-in-the-face-of-the-world attitude. Henry was not unsympathetic. Though he seldom admitted it to himself he missed Rosalie, or at least he missed her type, the openness, the sexual abandon, the irresponsibility. He had carefully avoided women of her ilk during the years he was rising in management. He knew how easy it would be to make the same mistake again. He knew what he wanted in a wife, a corporate wife, one of whom he could be proud, one with her own life and business interests. Mona fit the bill perfectly. Still, sometimes when he remembered his first weeks with Rosalie, he ached.

The night before Carin arrived Henry sat up late in his study. He made a list of his accomplishments. He had over $70,000 in the bank. He was a valued employee, managing a large branch office; in two or three years he would be promoted into senior management, with a move to either Los Angeles or San Francisco as part of the promotion. His large home was nearly paid for, there were investments to see him to and past retirement. His life lacked nothing of a material nature; he and Mona each owned an expensive car; Vaughan attended a select private school; last year the family had enjoyed a skiing vacation in Switzerland. He had a devoted wife, a charming son. He drew a diagonal line through the list. He wrote the word CARIN in the middle of the page below the list. He had never felt such love for another person.

Carin arrived on the 10:00 A.M. flight. As Henry Vold waited by the United Airlines baggage carousel, he felt the familiar spasms of love expand his chest. When he saw her he hurried toward her, smiling. She was of his own flesh and he felt as if she was the only person in the world who was. She was the little girl who hugged his neck and trusted him implicitly. Did fathers always consider their daughters to be little girls, he wondered? She did not see him yet, and he studied her as she approached. She tossed her head, a familiar gesture, swinging her long, sun-bleached hair back off her face. She was 16, but certainly to strangers she looked older. Tall and tanned, she wore blue jeans and a matching denim jacket, with a yellow sweater underneath. Yellow was her favorite color.

In the first instant that he embraced her Henry could feel a stiffness about her, a reluctance – her back was straight as a rake. Perhaps she was expecting him to be angry.

He kissed her cheek and whispered, "I love you," and she relaxed in his arms, embracing him as she had as a child, burying her face in the crook of his neck. He breathed easier; Carin was home.

Her eyes and hair were golden and she had traces of his own reddish coloring. She was nearly as tall as he was; he noticed that her pale fingers were long and thin as pencils.

"I've missed you, Daddy," she said.

Henry knew that Mona was apprehensive about Carin's arrival. He had kept his lives separate; Mona and Carin had met only twice; Carin had seen Vaughan only once.

But whatever it was that Mona was expecting: a sullen-faced delinquent mumbling monosyllabic replies to questions, an inno-cent possessed, a junkie, Carin was none of these. Considering the trauma she must have endured in the previous few months, she was bright, happy, charming.

"She's not what I expected at all," Mona said, the evening of Carin's arrival.

Henry had always, starting in the years when he had been a single father, traveled to spend time with Carin. They usually took a vacation together. They had been to Disneyland, San Francisco, Atlanta, Vancouver Island. For her 12th summer they took a cruise to Alaska. One Christmas Henry took her to the Super Bowl in New Orleans. They enjoyed discovering the tangy Creole food, but neither of them were football fans, and the rowdiness, the mindlessly destructive attitude of the fans appalled them.

"She's very sensitive," Henry replied. "She's what I might have been if I'd been less disciplined, had time in my life for something other than business."

"She's only a child," said Mona. "You give her too much credit."

"I'll be able to handle her," Henry said. "She doesn't have any reason to disappoint me."

Though Henry never intended it, never consciously imagined it; from the moment Carin entered his home, becoming at least for the moment a permanent part of the family, alliances were formed. Henry and Carin on one side, Mona and Vaughan on the other.

Henry was secretly pleased that Rosalie and Alex had failed with Carin. He knew he was the only one who understood her, and, he thought, the reverse was also true. Carin was the only one who truly understood him.

It was early June and Carin didn't have to think about school again until fall.

"I'm never going back," she said, her eyes hard.

He knew she meant school, he also hoped she meant she was never returning to Rosalie and Alex. Henry hoped that by fall she'd change her mind about school. She had always been an A student, but this past year her grades had plummeted. Carin claimed she was bored by undemanding classes. Henry promised to look into alternative schools, somewhere where she could concentrate on her interests, which were reading and studying literature.

While Henry wasn't an avid reader; he preferred non-fiction, or an occasional spy thriller, he sympathized with Carin's interests. They spent time in his study with books; Carin read aloud to him from some of her favorite books, and, as she had done from an early age, let him read her poetry. She was particularly taken by the dark visions of death in the work of Sylvia Plath and Anne Sexton. She also read a playwright named Samuel Beckett, who it seemed to Henry wrote nonsense, and who he suspected of perpetrating a colossal private joke at the expense of readers and critics.

"Beckett writes about the nothingness that surrounds us," Carin said, "the emptiness and pointlessness of life. We all engage in empty rituals from our birth until our death," Carin said, her eyes dark.

Henry had never considered that life was either empty or pointless. The concept took him by surprise.

"People who work hard, who are busy accomplishing, don't have time for that sort of thing," he said.

Carin frowned.

He listened to her poetry with both a sense of pride at her achievement, and a sense of fear at what he was hearing. Her poems were full of images of death, darkness, destruction.

"There is a beast that hunts me down," one of them began. Her poetry was greatly occupied with the macabre.

One evening Carin brought home a book on birds of prey. They pored over it in Henry's study. Carin, he discovered, had a gift for figurative language, something else, he thought, that they shared, for he was slowly discovering that he was capable of seeing the world, as a poet did, in terms of comparisons. He was thrilled by his discovery, but shy to show Carin that he understood, afraid he might be imposing on her territory. He even tried writing a few poems, but he kept them hidden deep in a folder in his desk.

"This one goes for the eyes of its victims," Carin said. "Once the victim is blind, the bird toys with it, gradually eats it alive."

"Such a beautiful bird," said Henry. "Is it really so cruel? It sounds gory."

"It does what it has to do to survive," said Carin. "That's what I'd like to do to Alex," she said suddenly, "swoop in and put out his eyes," and she raised her arms and curled her long fingers into talons.

"Why do you hate Alex?"

"Because he's bossy and stupid, and Mom believes everything he tells her."

"You never have to go back there if you don't want to. Your mother can visit you here."

"I don't want to see her either," she said bitterly, then just as suddenly changed the subject. "Look at this hawk, it can carry things four times its weight," and she pointed to a picture of a fierce brown bird flying off with a small goat clutched in its claws.

Henry decided that if he spent enough time with Carin, if, without being maudlin or overly sentimental, he showed her how much she was loved, he was sure everything would work out. He took to leaving work early in order to be home with Carin in the late afternoons; he felt it important that they have time together before Mona arrived after picking up Vaughan at the babysitters. Henry had been adamant that Carin was not to have to babysit her stepbrother during the days.

"She needs time to adjust," he said. "She had to babysit Rosalie's kids, that was one of the many things she feels resentful about."

It seemed ironic to Henry that over the years even Rosalie had become domesticated. She eventually married an iron worker, a big hulk of a man with a beer belly and hands like baseball gloves. They had three children and seemed happy enough. Henry often wondered what life would have been like if he could have accepted Rosalie as she was. For it was at her worst that she excited him most.

On those late afternoons Henry often arranged excursions to parks or movies; he urged Carin to bring friends along if she wished. That was how he came to meet Evangeline.

She was in the living room with Carin one afternoon, and the first thing Henry noticed was that she was very beautiful in a wild, dishevelled sort of way. She was as dark as he and Carin were blond. Evangeline looked vaguely Mexican, though her eyes were green, oriental in shape. Her blue-black hair was long, coarse, and uncombed. She had dark freckles across her cheeks and nose.

She smiled a pouting, sensual smile when Carin introduced her. She was wearing jeans; a black T-shirt, and apparently nothing else covered her ample breasts. One leg was slung over the arm of an easy chair; she was smoking a cigarette. Henry walked across the room and shook hands with her. Evangeline's hands were large for a girl's, the fingers chunky and sepia-colored, the nails wide and square. Henry Vold shivered as their hands touched. Her nails were covered in chipped, cherry-colored polish.

Henry supposed she was 19 or 20 at the least, and was surprised to learn she would be in Carin's class at high school, when it opened in a couple of weeks.

"I told Vangy she should come to the movies with us," Carin said.

At the movie, one of the girls sat on each side of him. They were loaded with popcorn, red licorice, beaded soft drinks in closed, waxy containers. It was an early show and there weren't 20 people in the theater. He was surprised at one point when Carin lit a cigarette.

"You're not allowed to smoke in here," he said automatically.

Carin looked at him sharply, with mild contempt, he thought. He debated whether to insist she put the cigarette out. Decided against it. No one else seemed to notice. No usher hustled down the aisle to accost Carin. No irate manager appeared to ask them to leave the theater.

Henry looked sideways at Evangeline; her denimed thighs comfortably filled the seat next to his. Her hand lay carelessly on the seat rest between them. She had her legs stretched out, one scuffed cowboy boot crossed over the other. Her fingers were buttery from the popcorn. Evangeline licked the fingers with little short strokes of her tongue, as sensually as a cat. Henry watched her helplessly; when she was finished there was a small patch at one corner of her mouth that still glistened from the butter in the flickering light of the movie. Henry Vold excused himself and made his way to the washroom.

A few days later Carin came home wearing an expensive leather vest. At first she said it was Evangeline's, that they had exchanged clothes. Later, in Henry's study, she admitted Evangeline had stolen it.

"I don't have the nerve to do what she does, Daddy. She makes no secret of what she's doing. Just takes something off the rack and walks straight out of the store. I waited for her outside. A clerk came running after her, yelling for her to stop, but we just ran off through the parking lot. The clerk had high heels."

Later she said to Henry, "Daddy, anybody with street smarts knows that when a suit tells you to do something, even if that suit has a badge, you don't need to do it. Rules are made to be trashed," and she smiled at him. Henry could see his own eyes staring at him out of Carin's face. In a strange way he envied her.

After everyone was in bed, Henry took the poetry folder from his desk and tried to write. When feeling poetic he liked to think that the protestant work ethic sat on his shoulder like a baleful-eyed buzzard, one of Carin's birds of prey. He thought of sharing his writing with Carin. But it was so bad. He could think of no one who understood what he was feeling. He wondered what kind of boyfriends Carin had. Women, he thought, whether they want to or not, usually end up with men a lot like their fathers. He had been Rosalie's mistake. She now had a husband very like her father. He was very much like Mona's father, successful; he even resembled him physically. He wondered about Evangeline's father.

"Who knows," said Carin after he broached the subject. "Evangeline's mother has a new old man every couple of months."

"Her mom's a little dark-skinned, but she doesn't have an accent. Vangy doesn't know who her father is. She really envies me for having such a great dad. I know who my daddy is, and I love you," Carin said, advancing around his desk to hug him.

That afternoon he had caught his first odor of Evangeline, sweet and tart at the same time, perspiration and perfume. Her skin was dusky, her forehead glistened with her body oils. In the days that followed Henry often recalled that sensual, sexual odor, as he sat at his office desk or in his study. He enjoyed it when the three of them sat in the front seat of the car, Evangeline close by his side.

Though Henry tried every approach he could think of with Carin, none worked. Rosalie and Alex had been strict; he tried being lenient.

"I trust her to do the right thing," he said to Mona.

To Carin he said, "Be cool. Stay out of trouble. Try to keep reasonable hours." She smiled and agreed with him, hugged his waist.

She went out on a Friday night after supper and didn't come home until noon on Sunday. When she appeared, Henry tried to be calm and reasonable.

"I was at a party. It was late, I stayed over at Evangeline's. I intended to phone. I should have. I'm sorry."

Henry could think of nothing to say except the tired, "Don't let it happen again." He decided to say nothing.

Mona was furious with both him and Carin, but she said nothing to the girl. For Henry, that Sunday evening was like old times. He and Carin joked about the peculiarities of some of their relatives. They played Chinese checkers. After they adjourned to his study they talked of Carin's poetry. She read to him from Sylvia

Plath, what was probably her most searing poem, one called "Daddy." The intensity of both the poem and Carin's reading frightened him.

"I hope there's nothing personal in that," Henry said, making his voice light, jocular.

"It's only make believe, Daddy," she said. "One of the anthologies at school says the poem is really about Germany and the persecution of the Jews, and not about Sylvia Plath's father, or any father at all."

"I'm glad."

"I love you, Daddy," Carin said, and walked around the desk to hug him for a long time.

"Are you just going to let her get away with what she's doing?" Mona demanded late that evening. "She's walking all over you and you're not even mad at her."

"What good would it do to let her know that I'm upset," replied Henry. "Would it make you happier if I snarled at her and called her names? If I beat her?"

"No, but..."

"I know how to handle her."

"I think it's the other way around."

Henry turned away from her and feigned sleep. He felt as if he had been assigned to stuff a cloud into a suitcase. He knew something had to be done, but he had no idea where to start. He did feel strongly that if he handled everything in a rational, businesslike manner, it would work out for the best. His all-encompassing love for Carin couldn't help but smooth the way.

After school started Henry made a point of calling on the counselors at Carin's school. They told him she was an indifferent and hostile student. They were sympathetic, but could offer no solutions other than to keep close tabs on her, and monitor her activities.

The second time she stayed out all night, she arrived home at dawn, unsteady on her feet, smelling of both beer and marijuana. Henry said nothing to her except, "Go to bed." He stayed home from work and called a Crisis Line whose number was advertised in the Personal column of the newspaper. They listened atten-tively, asked a number of questions, eventually supplied him with the names of a couple of social service agencies who counseled families with delinquent children. He visited the agencies. The social workers were supportive and sympathetic, but could offer no solutions. A certain percentage of teenage girls became difficult or impossible to manage, they told him. Set down rules of conduct and behavior and enforce them. Keep a close watch on her and hope she didn't choose to run away.

Not very reassuring, Henry thought. Carin was, for the most part, two completely different people. Around him she was sweet and loving, but everywhere else she was surly, defiant, a trouble-maker.

Carin offered little resistance to the rules Henry proposed. He insisted that he know her whereabouts and who she was with. Instead of going out she invited Evangeline to the house, and, occasionally, a thin black girl named Tiffany, with narrow eyes and a monosyllabic vocabulary. Tiffany was the adopted child of white parents. The girls spent a lot of time in the recreation room watching MTV.

When she was going somewhere Henry insisted on driving her there, and picking her up afterward. He would drive her and Evangeline to a house party, pick Carin up at midnight. She was sometimes sullen when she first got in the car but her mood usually changed.

"I can give Evangeline a ride home too," he said one evening.

"Vangy doesn't have a curfew. She can go anywhere and do anything she wants."

"It's too bad she doesn't have someone who cares enough to keep an eye on her," Henry said.

"Do you like Evangeline?" Carin asked.

"She seems very nice," Henry replied.

"No, Daddy, I mean *really* like her? Evangeline likes you."

Henry had no idea what to say, so he remained silent. But over the next few days he looked more closely at Evangeline each time she visited the house. She was in fact an adult. She would turn 18 in a few days. There was a wild sensuality about her. Henry dreamed of filling his hands with Evangeline's tangled black hair. She smiled at him with her lips parted; she always sat next to him in the car, her thigh snug against his. I can't let myself be drawn into something like this, he told himself. She's a child. My daughter's friend. I have too much to lose.

But the next weekend when he drove Carin and Evangeline to a party, they invited him to come inside with them. At first he declined.

"My birthday was on Thursday," said Evangeline, and she coaxed him, as did Carin.

Henry felt like someone who was about to be swindled, who knew he was about to be swindled, but the con artist's pitch was so wonderful that he couldn't say no. Evangeline took his hand as they walked up the sidewalk to the house, and he felt like he was 16 again, on a first date, frightened but looking forward to every second.

There were perhaps 15 people sitting around the smoky living room. As the stereo pelted out rock music so loud as to make conversation impossible, someone placed a bottle of beer in Henry's hand. A couple of people nodded to him. No one seemed to think it peculiar that he was there with Evangeline. The young men ranged in age from about 18 to 30. The girls were all about Carin and Evangeline's ages.

Evangeline sat on the arm of his chair, then gradually slid down until she was seated on his lap. Her long, denim-covered legs were draped over the opposite arm of the chair. She balanced herself by placing her right arm around his neck.

Couples danced occasionally. Henry could smell marijuana, but everyone was well behaved. Across the room Carin was standing, left hand on left hip, talking with a raggedly dressed boy with long hair, ringlets touching his shoulders.

"Would you like to?" Henry shouted, nodding toward the dancing couples.

"No," Evangeline shouted into his ear. "I'm much too comfortable here." She tightened her grip on him as she reached across and put her cigarette out in an ash tray on the chair arm. Then she made herself available to be kissed, pulling Henry's head down toward her. Her tongue against his was like an electric shock. Evangeline pressed herself into his arms, hard. Henry found himself staring across the room trying to see whether Carin was aware of what was happening.

"You're uncomfortable with Carin here, let's go someplace else."

They went to Evangeline's mother's house, after Evangeline phoned to make certain she was not at home.

Henry was surprised at her expertise in bed. She was passionate, not surprised by anything he suggested. With Evangeline, Henry remembered the first wild months of his life with Rosalie. It had, it seemed to him, been many years since he had really made love. What he and Mona experienced were careful and planned, antiseptic acts performed on fresh sheets beneath the ever-present hum of the air conditioner. Suddenly, here was Vangy, open to him in every way, their bodies drenched with sweat, his shoulders stinging from where Vangy's nails had raked him, the room overflowing with the sweet odors of sex.

"I like being with you," Evangeline said. "Most of the boys I know are so dumb. And they think making love is like making a line plunge in football. I like being with a real man."

The call from school caught up with him at work. Carin had not been at school for over a week, was something wrong?

"But I dropped her off this morning," Henry said, "in fact I drop her off every morning.''

The school was insistent. The counselor came on the line.

"We've noticed that Carin has taken up with bad company,'' the counselor said. ''That girl Evangeline has a severe attendance, as well as an attitude problem. She hasn't been to school for over a week, and I doubt that we're going to let her back in. She also compromised one of the male teachers; I'm afraid when it's all straightened out he may be suspended.''

Henry was at home when Carin and Evangeline arrived at mid-afternoon. He watched them come up the walk, laughing and animated.

"The school called this morning,'' he said.

"Oh, Daddy,'' Carin said, ''we just couldn't stand anymore. Everything we were doing was so pointless. We're not going back.''

"We?'' said Henry. ''Does Evangeline's mother know about your decision?''

"Her mom's not interested in her,'' Carin said easily.

"My old lady could care less, as long as I stay out of her hair,'' said Evangeline, her throaty voice insolent.

"Well, I care,'' Henry said, ''about what happens to both of you.''

Henry didn't quite realize how it happened, but the confrontation drifted into nothingness. If Carin was someone I disliked I could probably have handled the problem, he thought. If she was an employee at work I would simply tell her to shape up or ship out. But if an employee quit it was no loss. What if he challenged Carin and she left home? Minor problems were better kept at home, he decided. Better to know where she was than to have her on the street in a strange city doing god-knows-what. It was his extravagant love for Carin that made him helpless to act against her.

And then there was Evangeline. What he had done was both foolish and dangerous, and his actions hung over him like a dark threat, though Carin was always sweet and congenial, never even hinting that she was in possession of damaging information. Her continued amiable nature, the joy they both took at time spent together, Mona called it Carin's ability to wind him around her little finger, somehow eroded the school-quitting problem. In fact, it turned from a problem to an unspoken conspiracy, for Carin continued to leave the house with him each morning, only instead of dropping her at school he let her out at a monstrous shopping mall, where she eventually met Evangeline and other of her friends. There was a library in the mall and Carin *was* spending a lot of time reading and writing poetry.

Evangeline called him at the office at 11:00 A.M.

"I was thinking about the other night," she said. "I enjoyed myself."

"So did I," said Henry.

"I'm home alone until four o'clock," said Evangeline.

"I shouldn't," said Henry, but he was already planning his day so he could be gone from noon to three. He could picture Evangeline sitting on the old sofa in her living room, her eyes sleepy, her hair a dark swirl across her face and shoulders.

On the way to Evangeline's Henry stopped at a department store where he bought Evangeline an expensive turquoise and silver bracelet. Walking toward the exit he found himself cutting through the furniture department, where he stopped and, staring around, found himself mentally furnishing a house. He imagined Evangeline beside him as they made decisions about chrome and glass tables, sofas, a TV. He remembered Rosalie and the fun they'd had buying used furniture for their tiny apartment. I'd like to be very much in love again, Henry thought. And I'd like to be starting over.

Two weeks later he became genuinely angry with Carin for the first time since her arrival. In a round-about way she let Mona know that she had quit school, and that Henry had known about it for some time.

"You're playing right into her hands," Mona said. "Can't you see how she's manipulating you?"

"You act as though you've had a lot of experience dealing with teenagers," said Henry coldly. "What do you propose doing?"

"First of all I'd stop all this daddy-daughter sweetness and light. She's just a kid, but that doesn't stop her from being a manipulative bitch. Look, it was no accident that she told me about quitting school. She knew I'd be furious with you, not her. If I'm angry with you, where do you turn for comfort? To darling daughter, of course."

"I don't think you're being fair to either of us," said Henry.

"She may not even consciously realize what she's doing, though I'll bet she does. She's just bursting with anger, toward her mother and stepfather, and toward you..."

Carin had once asked him about his initial separation from Rosalie. He had tried not to sound bitter; the problem, he explained, had been that Rosalie was too young, too immature to be interested in making something of her life, or to be supportive of him while he made something of his.

"She was not interested in making the sacrifices that success requires," he said.

"Wasn't she proud of you, Daddy? Grandma says you were the youngest man ever made a manager in your company in Cincinnati."

Henry laughed. "Your mom would have sooner had me unemployed, hanging around the house. There's a saying 'Beer and hard times' that applies to your mom and her family."

"Don't I know it," said Carin. "Her and Alex are losing their house to the mortgage company. And neither of them care about it. And their kids are brats..."

"I'm listening," Henry said to Mona. "How would you handle the situation?"

"I'd make it clear that kids who don't go to school get a job. Give her one of your pep talks on economics, productivity and returns. No work, no money for food, cigarettes, and arcades. Cut off her cash flow. I can understand that you feel guilty, but showering her with money won't help. Set a few rules for her and make her stick to them. If she doesn't, kick her out. Tell her to get some better-class friends. Have you seen the boys who pick her up? They look like thugs, and that Evangeline is pure trouble if I ever saw it."

"Evangeline's really quite pleasant," said Henry. "She's had a rather indelicate home life, though. A long succession of step-fathers..."

"Oh really," said Mona. "Trash is trash."

It was that conversation which gave Henry the idea of visiting Evangeline's mother, though when he set out he had no idea what he expected to accomplish. He certainly wasn't about to confess his affair. He went on a Saturday afternoon, when he knew Carin and Evangeline were downtown together.

"Are you Evangeline's mother?" Henry asked the woman who answered the door.

"Yeah, I am. But Vangy ain't home," she replied, swaying almost imperceptibly.

"It's you I want to talk to. My name is Henry Vold, I'm Carin's father."

"Oh yeah?" said the woman. She was around 40, wearing a garish, flowered housecoat. She had probably been pretty when she was younger, Henry decided. But she had let herself go; he thought of a used car that had gone through the hands of a dozen abusive owners. He noticed that the pupil of her left eye seemed off center. "Carin's a good kid," the woman went on. "Spends a lot of time with Vangy. Polite as you please. I really like Carin." She took a deep drag on her cigarette, and Henry noted that her index finger was stained yellow.

"Thank you," said Henry. "But actually we're having a little trouble with Carin. She's very headstrong. Insists on doing as she pleases. It's a worry with her being only 16."

Henry felt uneasy staring into a house that was supposed to be strange to him but wasn't. He knew the way to Evangeline's room, remembered the thrilling sounds of their lovemaking, the way the bed frame rattled.

"Yeah? She told me she was 18. Vangy tells everyone she's 18, but she's got almost a year to go. I'd like to be 18 again, and know what I know now." The woman laughed a cough-like laugh.

"Wouldn't we all," said Henry. He noticed that Evangeline's mother tended to run her words together when she spoke.

"Let's not stand out here," said the woman. "Come on in."

Henry followed her into the cluttered and untidy living room. A small child of perhaps four played in a litter of Lego and matchbox toys. Henry couldn't decide on the sex of the child.

"The place is kind of a mess. I was out late last night."

"No problem," said Henry. He knew the house was always like this. In fact one afternoon Evangeline had sat on the same sofa cushion he was sitting on now; he had pushed up Evangeline's T-shirt and taken one of her dark-nippled breasts in his mouth.

She switched off a fingermarked black and white TV, and sat heavily in an armchair.

"Hey, can I get you a beer?" she asked, picking up her own bottle from a cluttered coffee table, patterned with bottle rings.

"No thank you," said Henry.

There was a certain odor about Evangeline's mother, and about the house itself; one that Henry associated with poverty. Perhaps it was a combination of too little soap, too many cigarettes and too much alcohol, in confined quarters. As he looked at Evangeline's mother, her housecoat partially open, eager to expose her breasts, he remembered his first months on his first job with the savings and loan. He had been assigned to collect overdue loans. He called regularly on a family living in a shack near the edge of the city. The husband was an unemployed miner who was seldom home. Each day Henry spoke with the wife, a woman in her late 20s, with a wide, freckled face and blue eyes. She was always braless and usually wore a man's white shirt, the tails knotted across her belly. Cut-off jeans covered her wide hips; she was always barefoot.

The odor of poverty was strong. Half-naked children mewled in the dark interior of the shack. Henry was obligated to call on her though he, she, and his employer knew there was little hope of ever collecting any money. The woman – what was her name? Blanche? Beatrice? – often joked with him after she understood that he meant her no harm.

"Here comes my afternoon love affair," she would greet him, "the neighbors all think we got a thing going. Like they say, if we got the name maybe we should have the game." She would laugh and drag heavily on her cigarette. Henry understood that she was laughing at him and not with him, and he would squirm in his suit and tie and repeatedly adjust the brim of his hat as he made a half-hearted attempt to at least extract a promise of payment from the woman. In spite of the squalorous conditions, the woman excited him, and, had he known how to go about it, he would indeed have liked to have had the game.

"Vangy's the independent type, too," her mother said. "She's been in a little trouble, but never as bad as it could of been. At least she hasn't gone and got herself knocked up. I was 15 when I had Vangy's big brother. Dumb. Christ, but I was dumb. Thank god they've got the pill available these days. I marched Vangy down to the free clinic the minute she was old enough. '"Life may not be a bed of roses,' I told her, 'but you're not gonna get yourself tied down the way I did, not if I can help it.'"

"A wise decision," Henry said. "I did the same for Carin."

"There ain't much you can do for kids, you know. I worry a lot about Vangy, but I guess we just have to hope they outgrow whatever's botherin' them."

"You're right. That's about all we can do. I hope you won't think I'm being too personal, but I was wondering if you'd mind telling me a little about," and it took every bit of his determination to use the mother's name for Evangeline, "Vangy's father." Henry hoped the woman wouldn't ask a lot of questions, make a production of it. He had no idea how he'd explain his interest if she asked.

"I guess I don't mind," she said. She lit a new cigarette. "I took a course one time on how to be a bookkeeper. The guy was the teacher. I was 23 and I had two kids; still hadn't learned what caused them." She laughed the cough-like laugh again. "He was married, of course. All the good ones are married. You're married, aren't you? Carin says your wife's a real snob. Pardon me for bein' so frank. Vangy's father was an okay guy. He offered to send money to help out, but I said no, didn't want to cause a lot of trouble. I showed Vangy a picture of him once, but I didn't tell her his name."

"Thank you," said Henry.

"You're sure I can't get you a beer," Evangeline's mother said. She ran a hand through her short, uncombed hair.

"No, thank you." Henry stood up.

"Yeah, well if I can ever be of any help, you know. Drop around any evening and we can talk about it. Maybe go out for a beer..." She smiled. She had been *very* pretty when she was young, Henry decided.

"Thanks," he said. "I may do that." He tried to visualize her dressed up. She probably wore rouge and the lining of her coat drooped. He left her leaning on the doorjamb, smiling in what she considered a seductive manner.

As Henry drove away he realized that he liked Evangeline's mother. He liked her because of her resemblance to Evangeline, as a young woman she had probably been more beautiful than her daughter. If only life had been kinder to her. The visit confirmed the decision that had been troubling him for weeks, hovering about his head like a troublesome fly.

Henry was scrupulous about withdrawing exactly half the money in each of the bank accounts. He also took an amount of money equal to the amount in his company pension plan, which he had signed over to Mona in his letter of resignation. From the house he took only a few clothes and his car. Mona earned as much as he did; their obligations were minimal. He felt badly about leaving Vaughan, but only for a moment. Vaughan was, after all, Mona's child.

He stashed the money in a plastic grocery bag. He changed the hiding place in the car several times, settling for a spot in the trunk beneath the floor covering, protected by the spare tire. But what was he thinking of, he asked himself? He had nothing to fear from Carin, his daughter. And Evangeline, his...lover.

He picked Carin and Evangeline up at the shopping mall at noon. They had been talking with a number of unkempt boys while a ghetto blaster roared in the background.

"We're not going to the movies," he said as he steered the car into the freeway express lane. Carin and Evangeline looked at him expectantly. "We'll be in Amarillo by supper time," he said. "Unless either of you have any objections."

They did not. Both girls talked excitedly. He stopped for gas and bought a six pack of Pepsi. Carin searched the dial until she found a rock station.

They headed east toward Amarillo and Oklahoma City. We'll turn south at Memphis, he thought. He liked Jackson, Mississippi, but they might go all the way to New Orleans. He knew of firms in both cities that would be glad to have him. Or they might go all the way to Florida, winter there before making any decisions. He had time and money and freedom. What more could I want, Henry thought.

Vangy's thigh, through her jeans, was hot against his. As she smoked a cigarette, Henry watched her face in the rear-view mirror, the lazy green eyes, the sensuous mouth. Vangy's bare, grime-dappled feet angled across to Carin's side of the car. The girls giggled excitedly. Vangy's left hand lay limp, half on her own thigh, half on his.

Henry was already thinking of later, when they would stop for the night. He could feel Vangy's nails on his shoulder, taste her tongue, hear his own furious breathing.

This, Henry Vold told himself again and again, as Albuquerque disappeared behind them in the cool afternoon haze, was exactly what he'd always wanted to do. Although, as he glanced down at Vangy's sepia hand, it seemed to him that the nails, covered with chipped cherry-dark polish, curled frighteningly. Images of talons filled Henry's mind.

BILLY IN TRINIDAD

Yeah, those are the questions I get asked alright. Soon as people find out I knew Billy the Kid. 'How many men did you see Billy kill?' is the first thing they ask. Then they want to know about the baseball.

I'll get to the baseball. But first I'll tell you God's truth. I never saw Billy fire his gun in anger. He killed some men, no question about it, but not nearly so many as history gives him credit for. And none without good cause.

To be honest, Billy the Kid once offered to kill four men on my behalf. All I would have had to do was say the word. And if the circumstances had been different I might have. Billy did what he did out of friendship and a sense of justice, though I was about the unlikeliest guy you could ever imagine to be the friend of a famous outlaw.

Billy chose me as his friend. I suspect he did it because I never owned or carried a gun in my life, so I wasn't apt to shoot him in the back just to make a name for myself, the way that little cur Robert Ford did to poor old Jesse James down Kansas City way.

Havin' a famous gunfighter looking out for you ain't as wonderful

122

as most people would think. It was because I was a known friend of Billy the Kid that I got gutshot by an outlaw named Bourque in a saloon in the town of Trinidad, Colorado. And it was because of my getting wounded that Billy offered to revenge me by killin' four men. I first met Billy in the Good and Bad Saloon in Santa Fe. I'd come west from Ohio, hired by mail to work as a clerk in the Wells Fargo office. But my boss was a tough and unreasonable man named Dyck, who a few months later was shot dead with a silver Derringer by a madam, because he was abusing one of her girls. I was rooming at the Coronado Hotel, looking for work, and it became my habit to drop into the Good and Bad for one drink after my evening meal.

I'd heard that Billy the Kid was in town. I recognized him immediately as he came into the saloon, walking as if the floor was covered in eggs and he intended to cross the room without breaking any. He sat at a corner table with his back to the wall; he wore a yellow shirt, his coat open to show the glint of metal on each hip. When he got all settled at his table he stared at me until I met his gaze, then he beckoned me over to join him. Billy's eyes were pale blue. Like a bird, his eyes picked up every movement in the room; he watched everyone in the saloon, all the time. I was about to sit across from him at the table when he motioned me to a chair beside him. He indicated with a flicking motion of his right hand that if I sat across from him I'd block his view of the room.

"Name's Billy," he said, extending a small, dry hand.

"I know," I said.

"Don't know nothin'," he said, his eyes narrowing. He was fair complexioned, his hair sun-bleached, a well-worn cowboy hat was pushed to the back of his head. "You got a handle?" he said finally.

"Schneider," I said. "George Schneider, from Ohio."

"I'm from everywhere," he said, and considered me for several long seconds before his eyes dropped from mine and his face relaxed into a smile.

Where did he come from? Who was he really? At the time I didn't know much about him. And there weren't any libraries in Santa Fe. Even if there had been, Billy was present history and there wouldn't have been a word about him. All I knew was what I read in the 10-cent western adventure novels that turned up occasionally. They were written by Easterners who never set foot outside of New York or Philadelphia. They were the ones gave Billy his reputation. Then he had to live up to it.

Over the next week or two I learned a few things about Billy, like that his mother's name was originally Catherine Boujeau and she came from Kingston, Jamaica.

"My grandfather was a French pirate," Billy said one night. "But they hanged him, and my mama had to run for her life." Then Billy smiled, showing that his teeth were small and white. He polished his teeth with baking soda at least once a day. I saw him do it right there in the Good and Bad Saloon in Santa Fe.

Catherine Boujeau met and married William H. Bonney in New Orleans in the late 1850s. They moved to New York City and Billy was born there, in about 1859.

One of the things Billy didn't mention was that his father was murdered in New York by a man named Harley Henderson. He also never talked about his first stepfather, a man named McCarthy or McCarty. Billy, using Henry as a first name, signed both those last names at various times.

No, he wasn't illiterate. I can vouch for that. Billy could sign his name, and I seen him write down and add a column of figures. And one night a big woman in a bustled dress and a blue bonnet came waltzing into the saloon and started preaching salvation to us sinners. She was waving her Bible in one hand and shaking her fist at the ceiling, when Billy caught her eye and motioned her over. He didn't say anything directly to her, just opened up the Bible and read out the first few verses of Matthew 6, which in a nice way tells loudmouths to mind their own business. That woman huffed and puffed for a minute or two but then she went on her way.

I'm told that over the years Billy signed his name William Bonney, Henry Bonney, Henry McCarty, Henry McCarthy, and Henry Antrim. Personally, I never heard him refer out loud to himself as anything but Billy.

Did he try to become famous? I don't think so. As far as I could tell he had fame thrust on him because our country was desperate for heroes, just as it's always been. Billy was a born underdog. He was small and lean, delicately constructed. He made fearless eye contact with anyone and everyone. It's common fact that prolonged eye contact brings on conflict. And Billy, in spite of his diminutive size, never backed down from a fight. Oh, he had a belligerent streak alright. He was a killer when he had to be, no doubt about that, no way to sweeten something like that up, but then life was cheap in those rough and tumble mining and cattle towns. Billy looked the part of a killer. I think that had a lot to do with why he became famous. He looked cold blooded. Still, Billy was always clean and polite, true to his friends – too true some say. I have no doubt that after I saw him for the last time, after I headed back here to Cincinnati, Ohio, where I married the girl next door and settled down, that Billy killed those two renegade lawmen who ambushed a friend of his. For after all, if I'd said the word Billy would have killed four men on my behalf, and I didn't even die.

I do believe I was the only friend Billy had during those couple of weeks in Santa Fe. Everyone else just sat around and stared.

"A gunfighter's the loneliest man on earth," he said to me one night.

"I'm laying low," he said on another occasion, "too many gunfighters, too many lawmen, too many New York cowboys want to make an instant reputation for themselves."

No, sir. He never denied who he was. I seen with my own eyes that he signed the register at the Coronado Hotel with the name Henry Antrim. William Antrim was the man his mother had married when Billy was about 14. A year Billy broke a chair across

Antrim's head and rode off to Pecos County, New Mexico, to make his fortune.

I was the one who moved on to Trinidad, Colorado. If it hadn't been for me Billy probably never would have gone there. I heard there was a bank clerk's job open and took the stagecoach down. Trinidad was 12 miles across the border from New Mexico, a mining town of 2500 people. I got a room at a rooming house a few blocks from the center of town, and each evening I would drop into the bar of the Columbian Hotel for my customary drink. To the local people the downtown area was known as Corazon de Trinidad, the heart of the trinity.

There were a lot of drifters in those days, information traveled, whether you wanted it to or not. So I was hardly settled in town before word got around that I was a friend and cohort of Billy the Kid. The job at the bank fell through and I was nearly broke. I allowed as how I'd give myself a week to find work in Trinidad. If I didn't I planned to move to Denver.

"There's a guy in town, looks mean as a mornin' after, and he's asking after the whereabouts of Billy the Kid," the bartender at the Columbian told me the second week I was in town. "Says his name's Bourque."

An hour later Bourque appeared at my table, towering over me like a giant shade tree. He was roughly dressed in a mackinaw and wide-brimmed leather hat. He looked more like a teamster than a gunfighter.

"I hear you're a friend of the Kid's," he said. He sported a three-day beard and his eyes were bleary from drink.

"I am," I said. I could see no point in denying it.

"He's a polecat," Bourque said. "And so are you."

He took a step backward, elbowing his coat aside. His hands were poised over his tied-down weapons.

"I don't carry a gun," I said. "Look!" and I went to open my coat to show I was unarmed. I'll never know whether Bourque actually thought I was going for a gun, or whether he used my movement as an excuse to enhance his reputation by killing a friend of Billy the Kid.

He drew on me and the next thing I knew the air was thick with gunpowder and I was lying on the floor feeling as if I'd just been kicked in the belly by a horse. The bullet hit my lower left side, slamming me and my chair over backwards. I writhed on the sawdust-covered floor, the taste of blood and the fear of death heavy in my mouth.

What happened in the next few minutes is rather like a dream. I was there, but I wasn't. Everything was veiled by the red haze of pain that closed around me like an evil cloud.

I could hear Bourque defending himself, saying I tried to draw on him, claiming self defence, repeatedly pointing out that I was a friend of Billy the Kid, as if that made me fair game for anyone with a gun.

I found out very quickly that a wounded man is a liability to any business, especially a saloon.

"Get out!" the bartender said, his face wavery and distorted as it stared down at me.

I was pulled to my feet, hurried through the saloon toward the street, my shoes not touching the floor. Outside the batwing doors, I swayed drunkenly on the sidewalk, clutching my side, blood dripping through my fingers.

I staggered dizzily toward the rooming house, but was overtaken by a deputy sheriff who spun me around and pointed me toward New Mexico.

"Get out of town," he rasped. "Sheriff don't want any outlaws dying inside the town limits."

I weaved off into the night. A couple of dogs skulked after me, whining, stopping to lick my blood from the dust. I had no idea where I was going or what I was going to do. At the edge of town I came across an abandoned adobe hut. Its sagging door stood ajar. I squeezed in, and by using all my strength was able to force it closed behind me, leaving the dogs outside. I collapsed on the cool, earthen floor. The last sounds I remembered before I drifted into unconsciousness were the dogs scratching and sniffing at the door.

Don't worry, I'll get around to what this all has to do with Billy. But right then I couldn't get around to anything. I figured myself for a goner. I lay all night and well into the next blazing day on the dirt floor of that adobe hut. My cheek was right against the cool, musty-smelling earth. I was too weak to move; my wound had dried but only after I'd lost an enormous amount of blood. My body sweltered with fever, my lips were dry as tree bark, my eyes burned as if I'd been staring into a bright sun.

I was too weak to even crawl. I knew I'd be dead in a few hours. It must have been late afternoon when I heard children's voices. I tried to call out but all I managed was to groan and cough feebly, enough to set my wound to bleeding again. I heard the door scrape open and saw the dark face of a boy above me.

"You hurt, Mister?" the boy asked.

"Doctor," I managed to gasp.

"You the outlaw?" I could see that there were several other children peering into the room, their faces black and indistinguishable, cast against the brilliant slash of sky behind them.

I had a whole speech I wanted to make. "No," I wanted to say. "What does it matter who I am, just get me help." But I had to work my mouth like a landed fish just to croak out the single word "Money." Using all my strength I pulled a few crumpled bills from my pocket and let them fall onto the packed dirt floor.

The boy scooped up the bills and disappeared. I faded in and out of consciousness. Darkness fell. I became very cold. My teeth chattered uncontrollably. Purple-winged birds flew at me in waves, their beaks clenching and unclenching like shears.

The heat of the day was on me again when the boy reappeared, in his wake a wavering black shadow.

"This here's Sister Blandina," the boy said.

"Doctor?" I whispered.

"Doctors don't treat outlaws in this here town," the boy said. "I tried every one of 'em, all four."

I closed my eyes and resigned myself to die.

The next time I awoke someone was applying a wet cloth to my blistered lips. I was wrapped in a blanket and there was a pillow under my head. The boy was nowhere to be seen, but the sturdy body of a nun was bending over me.

"Do you haff a name?" she asked.

"Schneider," I said with some difficulty.

"Cherman?" she said.

I didn't have strength enough to speak again, but I forced myself to nod.

"I used to be Cherman," she said. "Now I am Sister Blandina."

It took three days for my fever to break, and as near as I can remember Sister Blandina stayed with me most of that time. She said she was afraid of what the sheriff might do if he found out I was still alive and in Trinidad, and for that reason she deemed it best not to move me to the convent. Instead, she brought a coal oil lamp, a packing box for her to sit on, more blankets, and medicine.

"I traindt as a nurse in Chermany," she told me. And I'm sure she did. She dressed my wound, and fed me various concoctions, some of which looked and tasted a lot like creosote. Either she or the boy who first discovered me, brought food every mealtime for a week. By that time I was able to sit up and even ventured a step or two on wobbly knees. Another few days and I would have been well enough to ride the stage to Denver.

It was the day after I first walked that Billy showed up.

The boy, Simon, who was one of Sister Blandina's orphans, pushed into the hut late one afternoon.

"There's a man in the saloon at the Columbian, says he's Billy the Kid, and he's mad as a wet hen. Wants to know what happened to you. He thinks you're dead, but he wants to give your body a decent burial. The sheriff and his deputy have suddenly been called out to the desert on business."

"Bring him here," I told Simon.

Sister Blandina arrived about the same time as Billy. On the way from the saloon, Simon had told of his unsuccessful attempts to get me medical treatment.

"I'm mighty grateful, Sister," Billy said. "I know there's no way I can repay you for saving my friend's life. If you'd allow me, I'd be happy to contribute to your good works," and Billy took out a roll of currency and peeled off several bills.

"The vorkers off the Lord are always in needt," Sister Blandina said as the bills disappeared onto her person. "Ve thank you."

Billy smiled like a choirboy and announced his intention to wipe out the medical practitioners of Trinidad, Colorado. He had learned their names from Simon, and quoted them back: Dr. Michael Beshoar, Drs. Charles and Oscar Menger, and Dr. Henry K. Palmer. Someone had pointed out Dr. Beshoar as he strode down the sidewalk in front of the Columbian Hotel. He was a portly man with gold-rimmed glasses.

I assured Billy that he did not have to kill the doctors on my behalf, though I did it quietly, not wanting for him to direct his ire in my direction.

"I'll wait a few days," Billy said, holding one of his silver guns in front of him, on the upturned palms of his hands. "I'll see Schneider here safely out of town and then I'll take care of them."

"Though repayment off goot vorks iss nefer necessary, I haff decided how you may, if you vish, repay me, Mr. Kid," Sister Blandina said to Billy. "I vill off course return your money," and the bills reappeared in her large hand, as if by magic.

"How's that?" asked Billy.

"You vill, ass a favor to me, spare the lifes off the doctors. Vhat they did vas wery wrong, but they are badtly needed in this town. I ask nothing more off you."

Billy reholstered his gun. He studied Sister Blandina for a moment.

"Very well, Sister," he said. "Your price is small. You have my word that I won't kill the doctors for refusing to treat my friend Schneider. And of course you may keep my donation." Billy smiled again, but though his face glowed like an angel's, his eyes were bullet-cold.

Sister Blandina said I was well enough to be moved, so Billy hired a wagon and transported me to a rooming house in West Trinidad, where he had rented us adjoining rooms. Across the street was another large rooming house operated by the Madam's Association for Recuperating Employees.

"Just say the word and I'll kill them doctors," Billy said that evening.

"And Bourque?" I asked, trying to deflect his attention.

"What goes around comes around," Billy replied calmly. "Folks at the Columbian say he's headed for Durango. Left without ever knowin' I was on my way to Trinidad. Too bad. But our paths will cross; I'll eventually kill him, if somebody don't beat me to it."

"Gunfighters have a limited life expectancy," he added, smiling wistfully.

"As do friends of gunfighters," I said, my fingers running gingerly across the still tender area low on my left side.

Only other person who knows about the fawn except me was a little girl, daughter of the owner of the rooming house we stayed at. Billy'd been out riding in the hills up toward Fisher's Peak, and as he was coming home he frightened a doe and her fawn that had strayed down from the hills for a drink at the Purgatory River.

"Fawn stepped in a prairie dog hole as she turned and bolted from the riverbank," Billy said. "Could hear her leg snap from 20 yards away."

I guess I looked at him kind of funny when he took out his knife and cut his pillowcase into strips. He was starin' around the room searching for something wooden he could use for a splint. Turned out he'd carried the fawn home across his saddle and stashed it in a shed behind the rooming house. We went out there together, me carrying the kerosene lamp from my room, and Billy found a wooden slat of some kind that he broke in half and made a splint out of. The little girl, the landlord's daughter whose name was Margaret, found us there. She went out and picked some grass for the fawn.

I'll always remember that evening, not just because I saw a man with a reputation as a cold-blooded killer wince in sympathy to the fawn's pain as he doctored that broken leg, but because that little dark-eyed girl in her ankle-length dress, who must have been all of eight years old, went out into the pitch black night and plucked armfuls of grass to feed and comfort the fawn. When the fawn was bedded down Little Margaret went back outside and gathered flowers and mixed them in the hay.

"They'll be a surprise," she said real seriously, "just like when I find raisins in my porridge."

I don't think the rooming-house owner ever knew we had the fawn hidden in his shed. Billy, me, and Little Margaret fed and watered and exercised it until the leg healed. Billy he spent hours teaching it to walk again. That fawn used to follow Billy up and down the alley behind the rooming house, its nose right even with his knee.

"It thinks you're its mama," Little Margaret said.

Years and years later I was passing through El Paso with my wife and son when I recognized those serious, dark eyes of Margaret's in a grown woman's face. We were in one of the best restaurants in El Paso.

"Excuse me," I said, walking over to the table where she was lunching with two expensively-dressed women, "but did you ever mix flowers into a pile of hay in a shed in Trinidad, Colorado, as a surprise for a fawn rescued by Billy the Kid?"

Her friends looked at me like I was a madman, but she smiled and said, "I reckon I did, and I guess it liked the black-eyed susans best.'' Turned out she were married to a merchant named Johnson and had two little girls of her own.

When that fawn was fully recovered and able to fend for itself, Billy took it down to the banks of the Purgatory and set it free.

After a couple of weeks, though my strength was slow to return, I was in no danger of dying. I told Billy repeatedly that he didn't need to stay in Trinidad on my account. But he just smiled and said he was enjoying the restfulness of the town.

"Nice to be in a place where, when I mind my business, the law minds theirs. I reckon I'll get back to serious matters soon enough.''

Oh, yes, the baseball. It's not true that Billy shot a ball that was in play. Oh, I've heard the rumors – that he shot down a ball, one that was going 10 feet over his head at shortstop – a sure base hit – that he shot it down and as it hit the ground he shot it again, sending it on one hop to the second baseman for a force out. That never happened, though I can't deny that Billy did wear both his guns while he played shortstop.

In mid-September a tall, hollow-eyed man in a tight-fitting black suit, got off at the Santa Fe Depot, pushing a tin trunk in front of him and clutching a hundred or so handbills in his pale, talon-like fingers. He was gone on the next afternoon's train, but overnight he tacked up handbills in every suitable and unsuitable spot in Corazon de Trinidad, advertising that on October 7, 1880, at one o'clock in the afternoon, a barnstorming baseball team captained by Chicago's King Kelly, who, along with player-manager Cap Anson had led Chicago to the National League championship with a 67-17 record, would appear in person in Trinidad, Colorado. Their pitcher was Larry Corcoran, who had a 43-14 record that year. Their back-up pitcher was a rookie named Charlie Radbourn, who over the next 11 years would win 308 games and become known as Old Hoss Radbourn. They also had a 19-year-old kid named Pete Browning, who wouldn't break into professional baseball for two more years, but would, because he hailed from Louisville, Kentucky, become known as The Louisville Slugger and have a million baseball bats named after him.

The handbill went on to say that this barnstorming team would, on their post season tour of the South West, take on the best local team available.

The stranger spent his one night in Trinidad at the Columbian Hotel, and it was in the saloon after supper that Billy caught his eye and beckoned him over to our table.

"Hey, Mr. Baseball Man," he said, "someone should tell you that there ain't no baseball played in Trinidad, Colorado. There ain't a baseball diamond in the whole valley."

"A problem that I am here to solve," the stranger said. His dark form was hunched vulture-like over our table. "You look like young men who have known the thrill of competitive baseball. I can tell by your accents that you emanate from the East."

"I've played a little," said Billy. "In New York my daddy and I used to watch games of a Sunday afternoon, and I played as a schoolboy in Indianapolis, but never since I came west."

"A shortstop, I suspect," said the advance man.

"How'd you know?" said Billy, his voice sharp.

"I know a man with quick hands when I see one," the tall man said. Then he turned to me. "And you, sir, an outfielder?"

"I'm from Cincinnati," I said, "and I don't consider that the East. But, yes, I was raised on baseball. I've watched a lot. In fact I've seen King Kelly many times when he wore a Cincinnati uniform. And like Mr. Bonny here, I've played a time or two."

If the advance man had any idea he was sitting beside Billy the Kid he did not let on.

"Then you gentlemen should have no trouble recruiting a team to challenge Mr. Kelly's All-Stars. I've already convinced Mr. Peckinpaw, the dry goods merchant, to construct a baseball diamond. He hails from Providence, Rhode Island, and was much involved with baseball before he came west to seek his fortune."

"I don't know," said Billy doubtfully, "the miners are mainly from Europe, or Mexico. There aren't many people in Trinidad who know much about baseball."

"Then show them," said the stranger. "Put on a demonstration if you have to. You have three weeks to raise a team, and there's money to be earned. I calculate that 2000 people will attend the game at 25 cents a head. One third of the gate to your team if you lose, two-thirds if you defeat Mr. Kelly's All-Stars."

The next day two men with a team of horses and a scraper began to level land and create a baseball field on the edge of Trinidad, along the gravelly banks of the Purgatory River. They scraped away the yucca plants, sage, and blade cactus, the wild sunflowers and spears of Indian paintbrush. When the field was levelled, Billy and I measured out the distances, showed Merchant Peckinpaw's men where to build a backstop.

Merchant Peckinpaw ordered baseballs, gloves and bats from the East. But once the baseball field was there and available for play, even though it was set on sandy river-bottom land where there was no lush grasses for outfielders to scamper on, no stately elms to cast shade along the baselines, a remarkable thing happened. We had barely imbedded a piece of planking in the earth to serve as home plate, when a middle-aged man, a clerk for the Santa Fe Railroad, arrived at the field, a bat on his shoulder, a glove on his hand. He was nervously tossing a brownish baseball with scarlet stitching from hand to glove to hand.

Two evenings later we had enough players for a pick-up game. Another ball appeared, and then another, dredged up like memories from the bottom of a trunk or carpet bag. Someone displayed another bat, this one hand-carved from a piece of wagon tongue.

A squarely-built Polish blacksmith, and his equally sturdy son stood shyly on the sidelines. When Billy approached them, the father, by sign language indicated they would both like to play. They spoke not a word of English between them, but by the end of the evening the father, whose name may or may not have been Stash, was able to clout the ball deep into the sunset where it often landed in the desert beyond the furthest outfielder.

There's one other story about Billy – one I can't confirm, but it was told by Sister Blandina, who wrote down her memories of Billy shortly before she died. It seems that a few months after the baseball game Sister Blandina and two or three other nuns were riding the stage back to Trinidad after a visit to Santa Fe, when they heard gunfire and the stage ground to a halt. A masked horseman, who Sister Blandina immediately recognized as Billy, called for everyone to get out of the stage and deposit their valuables on a saddle blanket that had been spread on the ground.

"You vould rob the servants of God?" Sister Blandina report-edly said.

"Of course not, Sister," Billy said, "you and your friends may stay in the coach."

"A man who loffs small animalds would rob from his own kindt for money?"

"Sister Blandina claimed that Billy smiled over his mask, waved everyone back into the stage, and escorted them for a mile or more through the desert, all the while demonstrating his ability as both a rider and roper.

The day of the baseball game dawned clear and bright. The crowd was as large as the advance man had predicted. There was only one problem, there had been a derailment on the Santa Fe Railroad and King Kelly's All-Stars would be hours late in arriving. For a while it was feared the game would have to be called off, but the tracks were eventually repaired and the train chugged into Trinidad late in the afternoon. King Kelly's All-Stars were brought to the baseball field in a caravan of buggies.

The crowd was anxious for the game to begin, for the air already had a chill in it and the sun was low on the western horizon. The dour-looking advance man was with the team and was designated to be umpire.

From his position behind the pitcher's mound he eyed the ragtag crew that represented Trinidad. When he noticed Billy at shortstop, a gun glittering on each hip, he walked a few steps toward him, calling out as he did so, "You can't wear your guns on the field, Cowboy."

"I never go anywhere without them," replied Billy, glancing down at the weapons. His tone made it clear that the umpire had overstepped his authority. The umpire considered the situation for several seconds, then cleared his throat loudly and returned to his position.

There was still no work for me in Trinidad, and I had made it clear to Billy that I had imposed on his hospitality long enough. He had also mentioned that it was "time to get back to work." We both planned to leave Trinidad permanently the day after the game.

Along the sidelines the famous pitcher Larry Corcoran warmed up. King Kelly himself was going to catch that afternoon, a position he played only occasionally in the National League. The air was cool and bracing, the sky high and brilliant. There was a skiff of snow on Fisher's Peak, which rose behind the third base side of the field.

In final preparation for the game I hit grounders to the Trinidad infield. At shortstop, Billy the Kid, in a yellow flannel shirt, his baseball cap pushed to the back of his head, crouched ready to spring like a cat the second the ball left my bat. Behind him the sun was dropping, the sky already turning a fiery orange. Oh, I wondered about him alright. Billy in Trinidad, there on the banks of the Purgatory River, still a few hundred days short of his destiny, where, in a rooming house in Santa Fe, a bullet from Pat Garrett's gun would end his young life. Shadows blocked out his facial features, between the V of his spread legs the horizon flamed. I hit the ball.

APARTHEID

"The situation here on campus is analogous to South Africa," said McCubbin. "There are whites and there are blacks and as long as everyone knows their place...well, you can complete the analogy." McCubbin was tall, slightly stooped, with a shock of reddish-blond hair and a ruddy complexion. Because they had degrees from the same graduate school, McCubbin had befriended the newly-arrived professor, Kirkendahl.

"I assume," said Kirkendahl, smiling wryly, "that I am black."

"As am I," said McCubbin, "figurative though it may be. At the moment I am often able to pass as white, and may someday, if I keep my nose clean, be classified as white. You, on the other hand, will *always* be black. The University of the Prairies is not known to be a hotbed of literary or artistic endeavor. You're the first creative person they've ever hired, and, believe me, it was a struggle. There is a lot of resentment here against creative people."

"I assume you've argued that if there were no creative people, English professors would have no novels or poems on which to lecture and write obscure papers in doctoral dissertationese."

"A metallurgist doesn't worry about where gold comes from;

he just hacks, cuts, melts, and molds," said McCubbin. "I have a doctorate, therefore my writing plays is merely considered eccentric, an acceptable vice about on a par with sexually deviant behavior. But you, my friend, are *only* a writer. So be prepared." They were walking the halls of the English department toward Kirkendahl's office. It was his second day on campus.

"I know the feeling. Yesterday several faculty people dropped by my office to introduce themselves; every one of them asked 'And what is your area of research?' Their eyes nearly fell out when I answered 'I don't do research. I'm a fiction writer.'"

"Serves them bloody well right," said McCubbin as they arrived at Kirkendahl's office. "Ah, I see they've refinished your door." Kirkendahl quickly compared it to doors on either side of the hall; it was indeed a much lighter shade than most – almost blond, covered in several coats of varnish.

"You won't believe this," McCubbin went on, "maintenance wanted to redo all the doors in the department, but the fossil element protested, claimed the smell of all that varnish would upset their esoteric sensibilities. Result: doors are refinished individually when someone vacates an office."

Kirkendahl shook his head in disbelief. He had assumed that the monumental task of acquiring a Ph.D. would somehow make a person less petty.

The conversation turned to Eustace Sewell, the Department Head.

"Sewell's alright," said McCubbin. "A limited talent in every way, but he doesn't get sloppy-drunk or seduce his female students. He's a Reader's Digest department head: clean, loyal, bright-eyed..."

"Sounds like Old Shep," said Kirkendahl. "Now, tell me about my neighbors."

"Women and newcomers get the bad offices. You've noticed that your window looks out on a wall and that you're surrounded by washrooms. Chap before you got awfully good at making flushing noises in the coffee room. Entertaining fellow; he's opened a porcelain boutique in a new shopping center. Your neighbors: Dr. Furlong is tough as bailing wire, brighter than most of the fossils who have air-conditioned offices upstairs. Unfortunately she's a woman; she's black like us but won't admit it. Next door is Dr. Juniper; she smells of mildewed books and wears a hat, need I say more. Across the hall is Dr. Lal, our token East Asian. His specialty is the Metaphysical poets, and saying 'Good Morning' in a cheery voice. I'm sure that phrase is the only English he knows. Students claim his lectures are incomprehensible, but he gives high grades if they tape record his lectures, transcribe them, and hand them in as research.''

Kirkendahl had come to the University of the Prairies with a newly published novel, a new advanced degree, and a new wife. He met and married Esme while attending graduate school in California, and he never ceased to be amazed at her boundless energy, optimism and enthusiasm for life. They had been in town for 10 days and she had already joined a half-dozen organizations, made more connections and friends than he would in five years. At her church she was already on a committee who visited the sick. Esme wrote and published travel articles and poetry. To start her day she wrote five letters, at least one being to a stranger. She was forever enrolling in seminars on aging, parenting, divorce, prison reform; her curiosity was boundless.

At the university where they met she had sat in on his seminars; she never said anything, but it must have hurt her to see him fumbling his way through his classes. Of the two, Esme was the teacher. Kirkendahl accepted that he had been hired solely on his reputation as a writer. It was Esme who knew the intricacies of grammar, Esme who could analyze an essay, draw students into meaningful discussion. She had taught high school English during the 10 years of her first marriage.

He invited Esme to sit in on his fiction writing class. She was an immediate hit, and the class the liveliest and most rewarding

Kirkendahl had ever taught.

Kirkendahl enjoyed the solitude of being a writer. He was uncomfortable with both faculty and students. He learned to work in his office using only the weak light from his one window, for he could then lock his door and not have to answer it, not betraying his presence with electric light shining under his door.

He and Esme often joked about his discomfort with people. He refused to join the Faculty Club.

"How would I ever know who to sit with? If a group of colleagues are having lunch, should I join them? I'd rather sit alone, but if I did what would they think? But if I joined them I might appear pushy."

"Other people are too busy with their own problems to care much about yours," Esme said. Kirkendahl hoped that was true.

"Shame, shame," said McCubbin jovially, as they walked toward Kirkendahl's office. "I know who you are and I know what you're doing."

"What?"

"My friend, you can't say poop in your classes without the Department Head getting shit on his shoes. There are no secrets here." Kirkendahl tried to recall anything either treasonous or incriminating he might have said recently. "I know about Esme attending your class."

"That's no secret. Why should anyone care?"

"Should have had your class take a blood oath of silence," said McCubbin, shaking his head. "That sort of thing is not done, especially by blacks."

Kirkendahl argued that he came from an institution where anyone could drop in on any class that interested them. "Besides, old Foster Fraser had his mistress in his American Lit. class. I hear they spend more time talking to each other than teaching. And there are others…"

"But *they* are not black," said McCubbin. Kirkendahl was uneasy for a few days. He did not stop Esme from attending his class. No one gave him any trouble.

Dr. Gladys Furlong, his colleague from down the hall, was about Esme's age, 33, tiny as a child, of a wiry build with blazing brown eyes and bobbed black hair. There was an aura of fierceness about her and Kirkendahl, if not exactly afraid, was a little in awe of her. It came as a surprise when she tapped on his office door late on a Friday afternoon. They were probably the only faculty left in the building. She appeared slightly bewildered. They served on a committee together but were not particular friends. Her specialty was 17th century women writers, most of whom Kirkendahl had never heard of.

"I've just come from the doctor," she said. "I have to go into the hospital tonight. It's very serious." Although she tried hard to remain composed, a tear oozed from each eye.

"I'm sorry," Kirkendahl said, "If there's anything I can do, either personally or professionally..."

"Visit me," Gladys Furlong said, shuddering. She looked so small and vulnerable.

"Of course," said Kirkendahl. As he spoke he remembered a conversation they had had in the faculty lounge.

"You get so after a few years your whole life revolves around the 40 or so people in the Department. That's frightening isn't it?" Indeed it was.

"How I hate to visit people in the hospital," he said to Esme that evening as he recounted the incident. "Nothing makes me as uncomfortable. Even if I know someone well, a hospital visit is like talking with a stranger in a bus depot."

"I'll go with you," said Esme. "There's nothing to it. Did she tell you exactly what was wrong?"

"Only that it was very serious."

"It's better if she talks about it." Esme had hospice training, had taken a course on the psychology of illness and death. "People want to talk, they just need someone to draw them out."

What Esme said proved to be true. At the hospital Kirkendahl stood in uneasy silence as Esme and Gladys visited. He marvelled at the ease with which they became acquainted, found common interests in literature, the theater, the feminist movement. Esme forced the conversation around to Gladys' illness, and, it seemed to Kirkendahl, it was with great relief that she spilled out all the details.

A delegation from the female side of the English department arrived, led by Dr. Barbara Juniper, who introduced herself to Esme as Dr. Juniper, followed by "I'm the Medievalist," as if it were a visible facet of her person. To an outsider it would have appeared that Esme fit in well with these academic women. What Kirkendahl noticed was that the three visitors talked almost exclusively of faculty matters, as if by purposely excluding Esme from the conversation they showed their hold over Gladys Furlong.

But Esme chatted congenially, and outwaited the visitors.

"I'll come back tomorrow," she said.

"I'd like that," replied Gladys Furlong, and the two hugged, Esme leaning awkwardly over the high hospital bed.

Esme was the red-headed daughter of an Idaho forest ranger. She wore jeans and a soft plaid shirt to a faculty wives gathering.

"It was like the Attack of the Polyester People," she said later, laughing. "Some of them would be nice if they'd stop trying to imitate their husbands by talking in academicese and looking pained all the time."

Esme did go back to the hospital on each of the three days before Gladys Furlong's operation. "I'm going to check on her," Esme said on the morning of the operation. "She's due out of the recovery room at 11:00 A.M."

It was after midnight when Esme arrived home, exhausted but beaming. "She's doing fine. There was a big 'NO VISITORS' sign on her door, but I went and asked the head nurse if I could sit in the

room, and she was delighted. I just sat and read. Gladys pulled the
IV out of her arm once and I went and got a nurse. A couple of other
times I helped her when she needed to throw up. I'm going back
tomorrow."

Kirkendahl felt uneasy, though he envied Esme her involve-
ment. She was too trusting.

"Several of the faculty came around," Esme reported. "Dr.
Juniper, Elizabeth Watson, and, oh, Dr. Sewell and his wife
stopped by. I told them Gladys was doing fine."

Kirkendahl felt his stomach muscles grow taut. "Why did you
stay at the hospital so long?" he finally asked.

"I was needed," said Esme. "She has no relatives, no one, and
the hospital is understaffed."

"Still, it won't be interpreted like that."

"Someone was sick. I sat with them. What's to interpret?"

Kirkendahl made no answer. A sense of precaution, he decided,
was what Esme lacked. Needed or not, Esme simply did not
know her place. Somewhere in the distance he thought he could
hear McCubbin's evil chuckle.

During the next few days Esme spent long hours at the hospital,
while at the university Kirkendahl felt an air of, if not exactly
hostility, of repressed anger, sarcasm, emanating from his colleagues. Dr. Juniper and Elizabeth Watson who had always been
formally cordial, were now cold and wondered aloud how Gladys
was coming along and when she would be allowed visitors,
without actually asking Kirkendahl what he had heard from Esme.

Eustace Sewell was more direct. "Tell your wife to give
Dr. Furlong my best," he said, smiling through what Kirkendahl
assumed to be bared teeth. Kirkendahl was embarrassed. He
intentionally stayed away from the faculty lounge for nearly two
weeks, until long after Gladys Furlong was discharged from
hospital.

"Allow me to speak in parables," said McCubbin, after knocking repeatedly until Kirkendahl answered his door even though he

didn't have a light on.

"Please do."

"Jomo Kenyatta, the old lion of the veldt, used to carry a moonlight-blue machete, which he used to chop up Britons like a chef cutting beans."

"Sorry, I don't speak parable," said Kirkendahl.

"Perhaps I speak in allegory rather than parable," said McCubbin. "Who was it said 'The good must suffer for other people's sins?' Anyway, figuratively speaking, the machete is about to fall."

The next day Kirkendahl was summoned to Sewell's office.

"I understand your wife is teaching part of your course," Sewell began, smiling. "It's only a rumor, of course, but I thought I should check it with you."

"Certainly not teaching," said Kirkendahl. "She sits in on my class and contributes like any other student."

"I didn't know she was a registered student," said Sewell, feigning surprise.

"She's not."

"Auditing the course, then?"

"She just sits in."

"I'll have to ask you not to continue the practise," said Sewell. He went so far as to bring out a handbook of some kind, pointing out a subsection detailing who was and who wasn't allowed to sit in on classes.

"She contributes a great deal to the class," Kirkendahl said rather weakly. "She's a catalyst."

Sewell pointed to the handbook, obviously pleased with himself.

"I'll see to it," Kirkendahl said reluctantly, "but the class will be poorer for it."

"Be that as it may," said Sewell.

Kirkendahl went directly from Sewell's office to a class. It was of interminable length; Kirkendahl's mind wandered as students discussed some ridiculous Freudian interpretation of a D.H. Lawrence novel.

As he approached his office he could see something pinned to the door. He knew the essence of it before it became clearly visible. McCubbin had certainly gone to a lot of trouble; taped to the door was a photograph of Jomo Kenyatta, white eyes blazing from his moonshadow face, a book clutched in his fat black hand. At the bottom, in McCubbin's pinched handwriting were the words "The good must suffer for other people's sins."

Kirkendahl pulled a heavy ballpoint pen from his shirt pocket and lunged at the picture. His pen split the glowering countenance down the middle, ripping the photograph and tape from the door. He flung both to the floor and massaged them under his shoe as he searched for his keys. The stroke of his pen had created a long blue welt in the pretentious varnish of the door.

BUTTERFLY WINTER

"Magic is only something you haven't seen before," the Wizard told Julio. "Some things that happen to us every day, people from the other side of the earth might call magic. And we might be equally impressed by what they consider ordinary. For instance, I have heard there are places where the wizards can make it so cold men turn to marble before your eyes."

Julio recalled the wizard's words the first time he saw the butterflies darken the sun.

High in the sand hills above San Barnabas, where the cane fields petered out to rock as the elevation increased, where stubborn evergreens stood hunched over like serapied old men, was the place where the monarch butterflies spent the winter in hibernation. It would be many years before the outside world would discover this wondrous fact, though it was known and had been ignored by the Courteguayan hill people since the beginning of time.

The monarchs, large black and orange butterflies, with wing spreads of up to four inches, migrated each fall from as far away as Canada. Some years a hundred million of them made the dramatic journey across the U.S.A., lines of them intersecting, the main stream becoming larger and larger, vibrating like Halloween streamers. Pulled by some invisible magnet, they crossed the continent, eventually forming a Mississippi of butterflies that flowed like an endless pipeline over the ocean to Courteguay and to the evergreens high in the sand hills.

Once they arrived, the black-bordered monarchs folded their wings, attached themselves to a needle of evergreen, and rested until spring when they awakened and again formed a fluttering, 1000-mile conduit back to North America, an undulating, whirling sky-ride of color.

From the base of the hills the butterfly-saturated trees looked dead, as orange as if they had been singed. Travelers from San Barnabas stared up at the pale orange trees and remarked that they must suffer from dry rot or blight. Then the trees passed from their minds. The hill people knew the truth, but considered the phenomenon unremarkable.

The residents of San Barnabas were used to the whirling tunnel of butterflies passing over the city each October and April, but only the Wizard had ever had the curiosity to follow the golden horde to its resting place.

The first year the Wizard was rich enough to own a hot air balloon he hovered high over the endless tube of life, which from above appeared to be full of jittering orange smoke. The Wizard knew butterflies were so named because early peoples thought witches took on the colorful, mysterious form in order to steal milk and butter. The Wizard fantasized that these butterflies took their color from gold and that wherever they landed he would find a mine stuffed with indescribable wealth. The butterflies, he decided, restored themselves by bathing in gold dust. What he did not expect to find was the most tranquil spot on earth, a fairyland of sleeping orange evergreens.

The few peasants in the area respected the butterflies, did not even cut firewood in "the season of the sleeping sunshine," as they described each butterfly winter.

"Local farmers stock their wood in early fall," the Wizard reported back, "for they've found even the sound of an ax will cause some butterflies to fall to the ground. And those that fall from the evergreen needles die. If a tree is actually cut, the ground around it is papered with the silken wings of monarchs."

When Julio returned from America after the baseball season, heavy-hearted and arm-weary, he sat for days next to the cool stream that cascaded down the hillside next to his mother's house. His only movement was his eyes, which twitched involuntarily when the blue fish tossed themselves in the air like coins. His mother tempted him with pheasant pie, pickled pheasant, pheasant burritos, and something indescribable, a dish she had seen illustrated in an American magazine. She had carried the recipe down to the compound and had the old priest translate as he pressed his face against the chainlink fence that confined him. The translated ingredients included lampblack, and a small electrical appliance. The dish, which was supposed to *Chicken Alejandro*, turned out less than satisfactory.

"I am not going back," Julio sighed. "Baseball players may be well paid, but they are not idols; they are traded like goats from one farmer to another."

He mooned by the stream for another week, while his twin, Esteban, studied Latin at the San Barnabas Library and conferred frequently with the moth-eaten priest behind the chainlink fence.

Early one morning Julio heard children screeching in the hills above the house; he looked up to see several silhouetted against the sky like stick drawings. Each child's arms were extended upwards; they ran, pointing, as if flying invisible kites.

Curiosity overshadowed his torpor, and Julio languidly climbed the hill.

"The butterflies are coming," the children chanted.

Julio scanned the sky; it was pale as ice. The short grass on the hill was scorched yellow; the day would be white hot in an hour or so. The sky was blank as water.

"How do you know?" Julio asked the children, who looked back at him with the contempt the very young have for adults who do not share their intuition. Though Julio was scarcely a year older than the oldest, his clothes and manner tagged him an adult, and they automatically distrusted him.

"Everyone knows," a sullen-eyed girl in a sugar-sack dress finally replied.

"I can't see a thing," Julio confessed.

"It is sad to be blind," said the girl. "My grandfather is blind."

"I mean in the sky," said Julio.

"The sky, the land. Blind is blind."

"I can see," said Julio, meeting the girl's eyes. She was perhaps a year younger than he, with a colt-legged vitality. She had tiny breasts pushing like shadows against the white sackcloth.

"Really?" said the girl, Quita, a mocking smile on her lips.

"I see a terrible beauty in front of me," said Julio. As he said it he felt his chest tighten as if his ribs were taped. It did not emerge in the bantering tone he intended. The girl continued to stare at him with sad, dark eyes, her lips slightly parted.

Julio, who had learned to joke in a foreign language with whores and groupies outside each baseball stadium where his team played, could think of nothing to say to this girl in his native language. He felt as he did when the bases were loaded, the winning run dancing yo-yo-like off third. Reacting accordingly, he breathed deeply, clearing his mind of everything. He pretended he was on the mound, the translucent batter dimly glowing to one side of the plate, his only thought to hurl the ball to his brother Esteban. Hurl it without interruption.

Moments passed, the other children raced on across the spine of the hill, arms still pointing skyward. Julio stood as if in a trance; the girl sat down, pulled up her knees, hooking her long fingers in front of her ankles. Julio blinked, stared up at the sky, which was still blank.

"Are you one of the religious ones?" the girl asked.

Julio gazed down at her as man must first have gazed at fire. "No," he said. "But I am rich enough to buy you your heart's desire."

"No one is rich enough to buy anyone's heart's desire," said Quita, "especially mine. I want to fly in the body of a white heron, sleek and smooth as soap, piercing the sky; I want to see my moonshadow dark on the water below me. Are you rich enough for that?"

"No," sighed Julio, his lips parted, watching Quita's lips, dying for the touch of them, terrified of frightening her away.

"The religious ones talk of going to meet their leader in the sky. He walks on water and converses with oxen, at least so they say."

"I am not one of them," said Julio. "The priests are kept in corrals like cattle; the militia has orders to shoot the missionaries you speak of."

"I'm glad on all counts," said the girl. "They are not interested in now. They claim to wait for their pleasure in another world. I want pleasure now, *and* in the next world. Are you really rich?"

"Yes, I am rich. I have just returned from America. I am a baseball player."

"If you are rich, why are you unhappy?"

"Because I am lonely. My life in America is like being locked in an empty room for months at a time. And, I am expected to perform miracles."

"With loaves and fishes, like the leader of the religious ones?" asked Quita. And though Julio met her straight, innocent gaze, he could not tell if she was making fun of him or sympathizing.

"With my right arm and a baseball."

"I know about baseball," said the girl. "My father was Milan Garza. He has been honored by El Presidente as a Courteguayan Baseball Immortal. He died when I was a baby. El Presidente would not allow my mother to bury him; his body was taken away and is preserved in a glass case in the Hall of Baseball Immortals at the Capitol Building. I have never been there, but I am told my father stands as he did in the outfield, in his uniform, his glove on his hand, a holy aura about his head. I am told, too, that his eyes glow in the dark."

"I have never been to the Capitol either," said Julio, "though I am rich enough to go any time I wish. Rich enough to take you with me. But Milan Garza is a national hero. Even in America I am asked by reporters if I knew him. He played for years in America; why are you, then, so poor?"

The girl stood up and moved closer to Julio. She was barefooted and he caught the first odors of her: sun-sweet earth, but behind it something darker, muskier, like the scent of the deep-colored nasturtiums that bloomed on the shady side of his mother's house.

"He invested his money somewhere, in some resort promoted by El Presidente. It was lost, if we are to believe what we are told."

"But the honors. El Presidente made Milan Garza a Knight Commander of the Blue Camelia; I read about it..."

"You cannot eat titles, or praise, or adulation. My father was poisoned so he could be displayed in a crystal coffin at the Hall of Baseball Immortals. 'A dead idol is much better than a living one,' El Presidente told my mother. 'A dead hero can never disgrace himself in his old age, never support unpopular political causes, disclose his strange sexual preferences, his unacceptable drinking habits, or a poorly-conditioned body.' You should know such quotes. You should also know that if you become rich and famous through baseball, you will have a short life. Has no one told you that?"

Julio breathed in the sweetness of Quita Garza. He remembered the fortuneteller who predicted his brother's early death. No, no one had told him anything. But he was not very interested in death at this moment. He was in love. He felt weak. The white sky made him dizzy.

He took Quita in his arms and the heat she radiated through her thin clothing disoriented him even more. Her lips were soft and easily parted, and as they kissed she clung to him with a ferocity he had not anticipated. He thought of easing her down onto the scorched grass of the hilltop, imagined the silhouette their bodies would make against the declining sun. But their passion was interrupted by the softest of sounds; birds seemed to hush, the wind surrender. The sky darkened as the wild spiral of gold-and-black butterflies came into view; it looked like an onrushing, endless train hurtling by, hundreds of feet in the air.

"I want to follow them," whispered Quita, staring up at the velvet movements of a million wings. And Julio, gazing with love into the girl's long face and luminous eyes, could deny her nothing. She took his hand and they trooped along the spine of the hill. The river of butterflies soon arched from horizon to horizon.

All the remainder of that day, and all the next, the conduit of butterflies flowed over San Barnabas like an orangeade rainbow.

On the ground, Julio and Quita followed along; they left the city behind, crossed the flatlands to the foothills, and began a slow climb toward the timberline, where the air was calm and sweet.

When they arrived at the butterfly forest, millions of the silken-winged creatures were already covering the evergreens on the edge of the timberline. Still, millions more were arriving, seeking rejuvenation after their long flight over the ocean. There was such a profusion their wingbeats could be heard; the draft from these fluttering snippets tousled Quita's long, reddish-brown hair.

Julio and Quita watched, enthralled.

"The wings of those on the trees are closed like hands at prayer," said Quita.

"Do not give them so much credit," said Julio.

"Can *you* fly home from America on *your* own wings?"

"I cannot," he admitted. "Can you love a man who cannot fly?" And when she didn't answer, Julio took her hand, which was dry and cool, and pulling her to him kissed her. She responded, her tongue sweet and warm, exploring, like a butterfly itself, against his lips and teeth.

The butterflies blotted out the sun as they hovered, searching for a place to land. Though it was mid-afternoon, their shadows dispelled the violent heat of the day and it became comfortable as evening. Julio undid the single button at the back of Quita's dress, and she helped him pull her arms out. She unbuttoned Julio's shirt and suddenly her tiny breasts were against his chest, burning like hot coins. Julio bent his head and her nipples tasted salty; she smelled of rope, tanned leather, and the dark nasturtiums.

"You should know I am not a virgin," Quita said, as Julio pulled her down beside him in the sun-sweet grass beneath the butterfly trees.

"Unimportant," said Julio.

"My stepfather sells me to his friends, or strangers, when it is necessary," she insisted.

Julio covered her mouth with his, swallowing the last of her words, fitting their bodies together, locking them in passion, two puzzles completed by a single action.

"I have never made sex for love," Quita whispered much later, their bodies still deliciously entwined. "I never thought I would. Now, I know why couples moan in the night."

"I am glad my father did not have daughters when he was very poor," said Julio. "But I am rich, and home for four months, and you will never be touched again, except in love…"

"Oh, look," said Quita, for a butterfly had landed on her right arm near the elbow. Both her arms were locked about Julio's neck. He was still inside her, their bodies sweet with their blended sweat, their mouths ripe with the tastes of each other.

Then another, and another of the gentle butterflies landed on Quita's arm. Wings closed, they were no thicker than two thin swatches of silk.

"My back," said Julio. "I can feel them on my back."

Quita raised her head from the lush grass and peeked over Julio's shoulder.

"They have made us a blanket for the night," she said. "There must be ten thousand of them on your back. Feel their warmth."

As she spoke, thousands more covered them with their gentle color.

"Do they have hearts?" whispered Quita.

"I feel them beating like a million pin points," said Julio.

All that evening the shimmering butterflies covered every inch of the lovers until only the places where they were joined in passion and in love were not cloaked. They looked like a burnt-orange sculpture in some erotic museum.

"They will die if we move," said Quita.

"Then we won't distress them," said Julio, and again he covered her mouth with his, as butterflies settled on their closed eyes.

And there they stayed, down all the long, silken days of their butterfly winter, Quita and Julio, entwined in love, secure under the sleek blanket of butterflies, waiting for spring.

FOR ZOLTAN,
WHO SINGS

The first day that I was modestly coherent Madge took me on a tour of the wing, pointing out the patients. "That's Jenny," she said, referring to an old woman, who clutched, upside down, a naked rubber doll. Jenny was dressed in a garish green crepe dress covered by an apple-red coat. She carried an emaciated green plastic purse over one arm. From her slack mouth spilled squirrel-like sounds. Her blue eyes were blank as sky.

A twisted apparition of a woman advanced on me, one finger extended, shaking. Her head was cocked permanently to one side, and little ripples of fear crossed her face like waves of water. "It's alright," Madge said, "she only wants to touch you. That's how she gets her human contact. Her name is Kate." Kate shuffled toward me, her hand reaching. She looked at me as if I were covered with elevator buttons. Her finger pushed on my chest. Then she turned toward Madge and tentatively touched the wide green belt of her uniform. "She's been here over 20 years," Madge said.

"And that's Zoltan who sings," she said, pointing to a slim, dark man sitting rigidly on a pale leather chair. "Every night about

eight he gets up in the middle of the common room and sings a
song. He's never spoken in all the years he's been here. Just sings."

"What does he sing?" I asked.

"We don't know. It's not English, maybe not any language. He
just sings. No one knows who Zoltan is or where he came from.
Must be 10 years ago now that they found him wandering the
streets of Boston. Zoltan may not be his real name. It's what's
tattooed on his left forearm. He's on the patient list as Zoltan
Doe."

Madge is a redhead, plump and jolly, her uniform the same
apple green as the walls here.

Wouldn't it be nice if they didn't know who I was, if they
didn't know where I came from. They could look at me and say,
"He's the one we call the Professor, but nobody knows who he
really is." It would give me the freedom to start over.

But it is only a thought.

They, of course, found out everything they wanted to know
about me. What I refused to tell them, they pieced together from
credit cards, photos, library cards, driver's license and I.D. I had
actually filled out one of those white cards that come with a new
wallet listing my next of kin, doctor, minister, employer. Within
a few hours of my admission, everyone connected even peripherally
with my life knew what had happened to me. There is as little
privacy in the real world as here at the hospital, where wardroom
doors remain open, matches and sharp objects are prohibited.

I had planned to see some baseball while I was in Boston. A
lifelong baseball fan, I've never been to Fenway Park. I mention
this because I found that I am in good company at Westview State
Hospital – it is the self-same place that Jimmy Piersall was carried
raving and screaming, wrapped and cushioned like an egg in a
carton. On the wall behind the counter at the nurses' station is an
autographed photo of Jimmy. I have considered offering them one
of my publicity photographs, but what if they said no thanks? I'll
settle for autographing some copies of my book when I leave.

I had given a reading in New York, and was due to give a workshop at Boston University the following day. I never made it. Somewhere during that drive to Boston, something snapped. I stopped at highway rest areas and made wild, rambling collect calls to my family. I knew what I was doing, but couldn't control my actions.

I felt as if I were inside a fish bowl. Over and over, I searched all my pockets carefully, looking for my pens. They should have been there. I needed them to defend myself. There was a devastating pressure on me from all sides. Wooly-headed savages peered at me, grinning, jabbering. Their faces were elongated, distorted, arms long and snakey at the ends. One threw a handful of dirt and stones directly into my face. Another spat on the glass in front of me. Although my blood fairly boiled and I knew I possessed enough energy to control the universe, it was a terrible leaden-armed effort to roll down the car window.

"I think I need help," I said to one of them. "Would you have someone call the police?" The boy closest to me appeared to be under several feet of water. Yet his skin looked very dry. There were fine whitish lines on his cheeks and chin, his teeth were terrifyingly white. I kept exploring my empty pockets. What I must have looked like I can only guess. To illustrate my lectures, I often use bright marking pens of gold, crimson, ocean blue; markers fat as cigars with squared tips that stain. I had taken those pens and decorated myself like a savage; my face, shirt, pants, the white upholstery of the car, all looked as if they had been turned over to a preschooler with a crayon. One of the paradoxes of going mad was that I could see all along what was happening to me, but it did not really seem to be me, and I did nothing about it. The person who sat for 48 hours in a car in a vile section of Boston alternately screaming and meditating, was someone I was able to view objectively and remain almost totally uninvolved with.

"What do you want us to do?" the swarthy police officer said to me, leaning his face in the car window, displaying no surprise at the way I had painted myself in garish wonder. His statement made me angry. Surely he could see I was deranged.

"What do you usually do with crazy people?" I wanted to ask him, but instead I affirmed my plea for help.

"What kind of help do you want, sir?" the officer repeated.

What was happening to me seemed to be working on the same principle by which a toothache stops or an appendix pain vanishes in the presence of a doctor. I had mustered what little self-control I had left to ask for assistance. Now, because I displayed some measure of control, I appeared not to need any help. "Have you never seen a harlequin before?" I believe is what I said in reply.

The officers conferred, then suggested that they could drive me to a local hospital. They locked my car, made sure I had my keys and valuables. I kept searching my pockets for pens. Eventually, I saw them stabbed behind the sun-visor like so many bloody knives. It was too late to claim them. In the back of the police cruiser gliding along over the bluey streets of Boston, I sang fragments of hymns.

At the hospital, it is Madge who draws me out from a self-imposed silence. Medications calm the boiling within me. Still, for the first day at Westview, I said nothing. Vowing I would never speak again, I lowered my eyes, pretended not to be able to hear when the doctors questioned me. But Madge talks of her children and grandchildren as if I know them.

And I listen and smile to myself at how ordinary her life is, how simple her pleasures. I am haunted by my past life, haunted now by visions of my wife. Not as I know her, but as she was shortly after our marriage, 18, maybe 20 years ago. Half a lifetime ago. Spent, I lay on top of her, the musky smell of her rushing at me as our bellies part. "Do it some more," she says in a tiny voice. "I can't," I reply, intending to add, "right now," but not adding it. We turned away from each other, a pattern of silence established.

"Now, a writer like you has got to be able to play Scrabble," she says, plunking down the board on a table in front of me. "I've read one of your books, you know. The one about the man trapped in the mine. It was good. I really enjoyed it." She chats on and plays Scrabble with me with infinite patience. I'm doing things I know are crazy, but pretend are normal, defend as normal. I put down SULG as a word and refuse to change it, arguing first with gestures and then with words that it is exactly the word I intend to use.

A voice interrupts us. "Is he really a patient here?" it says.

The speaker, a bony woman with lank, blond hair and a ravaged face sidles toward me as she speaks, paranoia oozing from every pore. Her eyes are brown, bright as a chipmunk's, but several degrees out of focus. I wonder if mine are the same.

"He is," Madge assures, "but he won't be here long. His family will be taking him home in a couple of days."

"Where did he come from?" the woman wants to know. She speaks to Madge, but sits down beside me on a fuschia-colored sofa in the common room. She's staring intently at my neck.

"Why don't you ask him?"

"Iowa," I say quickly.

"Oh, they grow potatoes there or something, don't they?" the woman says. "Are you sure he's a patient?"

As we play Scrabble, Zoltan Doe sits nearby on a wooden folding chair, head bowed. Where does Zoltan come from? I keep glancing surreptitiously at him, forgetting the game. He must surely be a sailor. Zoltan is close to 40, I think, with short black hair, black eyes and an olive complexion. He is about 5'8" with a wiry body that carries no excess weight in spite of his years of forced inactivity. He looks as if he could scale a fence and run zig-zag for the forest while a guard took potshots at him from an observation tower. I picture us doing that together. I would sprint into the golden path of the searchlight, drawing the gunfire, allowing Zoltan to escape.

I see him wearing a squarish sailor's hat with crossed blue

ribbons hanging down just behind one ear. Perhaps he was a crewman on a Liberian freighter (aren't all freighters Liberian?) led ashore, abandoned like an unwanted cat by his shipmates because he had gone crazy. Does he have a wife and family in some far off place? Maybe he wasn't abandoned at all. He probably strongarmed his way out of a sick bay and fled ashore only hours before his ship was to sail. Perhaps the authorities have always meant to inquire about him further, but just never got around to it. As if on cue, Zoltan rises from the wooden chair where he has been sitting, back stiff, hands in lap. He marches to the center of the room and brings himself to rigid attention. He clicks his heels and I can hear the sharp snapping sound like the breaking of a dead limb off a tree. Zoltan is wearing only hospital-issue wooly slippers on his feet, but he can hear the sound, too. I can tell by the look in his eyes – eyes that are thousands of miles away from this grainy, too-hot room that smells of stale smoke, disinfectant, and floor wax. He is on a parade square somewhere and I picture him in the blue and brass tunic of the French Foreign Legion.

I wear my own clothes now. The first night, I was draped with a scum-green gown that bunched under me in lumps. I missed my own bed, my flannelette pajamas. I felt like an unpainted house. I wanted to cut my arms open and insert the tips of my missing felt markers and feel the color and brightness surge through my veins. I equate brightness with energy and change. There is no change for me. I have tenure. The rest of my life is mapped out for me. I am like a rat that has found his way through the maze. There will be no surprises now. We, my wife and I, are saving for our children's college educations; we will retire to a condominium in Florida. Already we own cemetery plots, and there is money saved for the transportation of our bodies.

I once read an interview with the famous singer Nat "King" Cole, in which he said he would give up his career as a singer, recording star, song writer and actor if he could play "a mediocre second base for a major league baseball team." It was considered a controversial interview. People said, "How could he?" and "Why would a man want to give up his fame for something like that?" But I understood perfectly. I've always had a similar desire buried in me, and now that I've attained a modicum of success as a scholar, teacher, writer, I would happily cast it aside for the opportunity to be a second-rate country singer. To climb onto a stage in the sequined suit and sing the old, old songs, the country standards, even in a small noisy bar or a country dance hall, is what I think would most fulfill my life. I don't know whether Nat "King" Cole had any talent as a baseball player, I have none as a singer. I can neither read nor play music.

I once told a colleague at the university where I am employed, "I teach nine hours a week and worry 44." I hear footsteps. I am afraid of my students. I know my colleagues talk behind my back.

In the middle of the common room, Zoltan's chin rises, his eyes stare up and off at a distant flag. Like a whip cracking, his right arm snaps out a smart salute.

"Uk, uk, uk." Sounds creep from Zoltan's throat and the image of groundhogs peering cautiously from their burrows fills my mind.

"Uk, uk, uk," Zoltan says again. Although there are only a few murmuring voices in the common room, I can hear music, military music. Then Zoltan begins to sing.

The first doctor who interviewed me had a face as red as a radish. "Nearly all my patients are depressed," he said to me, chuckling slightly as if he were eating peanut shells. "They're easy to understand. It's a depressing world. Manic episodes like yours, however, are more rare. What in the world do you find to get so excited about?" and he chuckled again.

I didn't answer him. His voice was so thin and far off, it was useless to even try. The medication made me feel stuffed with lead, limp as a string of sausage.

It was night when the ambulance delivered me to Westview, raging and screaming. I was medicated, "enough to knock out an ox," Madge told me later. I woke the first morning looking directly at a window. I could see nothing but sky. I could hear a strong wind blowing and felt very clever to realize there must be a tree directly to the left of the window. Although I couldn't see a tree, a brisk wind catapulted leaves across the window like yellow birds. When I stood up, I shambled like a wino, my ankles rubbery.

"You're making a remarkable recovery," the doctor tells me. It is due, in part, he assures me, to the fact that my friends and family have flocked to me. "Your wife and daughters were here within 24 hours. And we've had more phone calls about you in three days than all the other patients admitted this month." Significant others – who care, love, rescue – play a dramatic part in recovery patterns. I realize most of the other patients at Westview have no visitors, no one to care. "You'll be as good as new soon," the doctor said, as if that is something to rejoice over. When I was "good as new" I had a breakdown, skittered away from reality like a kicked dog. I still have the desire to, for once, do something unexpected, yet something I have control over. In Zoltan, I see my chance.

For three nights I've watched Zoltan sing.

It has become a monomania; at dinner, I sit for many minutes, my fork poised over a cutlet. All that interests me is Zoltan the mysterious singer of mysterious songs. I can feel myself recovering, for I can again hide my emotions – bury them as if they are corpses, dig little graves in my arms and lower them into the bloody depths, secretly, so no one will ever find them.

The other inmates pay little attention to him, serving only as a captive audience, or, like old Jenny, they pace fretfully, carrying on eerie conversations, their voices like starlings quarreling in a tree. Zoltan sings, remains at attention several minutes, then at some unheard command, he marches off to his room.

Even my untrained ear can tell Zoltan is off key. The language he sings is not English, or French, yet I am certain that what he sings is *La Marseillaise*, the French national anthem. He sings in a language incomprehensible to me, perhaps Greek or some Balkan dialect.

He sings the song twice, in a high, thin voice, his eyes staring off reverently at what? Some crisp green and white flag snapping in a salty wind? Then he brings his saluting arm to his thigh with a slap. He stands rock still.

My turn now.

I will sing the old Hank Williams' songs, the Hank Snow ballads I was raised on, some Willie Nelson, songs by Waylon, and Dolly, and Loretta. When I finish, there will be applause, and screams, and arms reaching out of the darkness toward me. Then, fiery little fish will swim in my blood. The high will last, and I will be able to breathe deep, stand tall, stride long, and fear nothing.

When I was 12, I took my newspaper route money and bought a guitar for 10 dollars, a cracked, stained instrument. To my horror I found I had no ear to tune it; I could not pick out even the simplest melody. How could I love something so much yet be so inept with it?

"We don't play that kind of music," my mother said. The collective *we* referred to her, myself and my sister, for my father was gone by that time, left in his 1949 Dodge, a few clothes and an apple box full of 78 rpm records of Bob Wills, Hank Williams, Hank Snow and Jimmy Wakely, his only possessions.

The common room has become my stage, dark except for dual spotlights that bathe me in an eerie blue light. The faces of my audience are invisible, their forms like dark stumps in a row. I can feel their energy pulling at me. My costume is white satin paved with red sequins, glimmering and flashing, giving off sparks like dancing fireflies. I hold my guitar as if it is part of me. It is custom-made, light as flower petals, and has many mother-of-pearl inlays.

But as I walk out there on the stage beside Zoltan, the words escape me. The old songs, *Half as Much, Take These Chains From My Heart*, even *Kaw-liga*, will not come to me. Instead, the words break loose, singly and in phrases. They flutter around me like butterflies, and like butterflies, completely elude my grasp.

From deep inside me then, like opening an ancient drawer and finding youthful treasures swathed in dust, smelling of mothballs, come words from my childhood. I remember being sick, so sick I was put into my parents' bed in the sunny south bedroom with its squash-yellow hardwood floor and white calcemined walls. Above the bed, a pin-up picture from the 1920s era: a naked woman sitting on the edge of a table. She looked a little like Betty Boop with bobbed black hair and rosebud lips. I never saw her naked. My mother painted on her body a bright, sky-blue bathing suit, again in 1920s style.

"She looked so cold," I can hear my mother saying when father chided her for her prudery.

Now on this lonely stage, I am able to grasp and hold to me, like a sobbing child, words my mother sang to me in that room.

Falteringly at first, in my tuneless monotone, I sing:

> Have you ever heard tell
> Of Sweet Betsy from Pike
> Who crossed the wide mountains
> With her lover Ike

I imagine that during those first lines the audience breaks into applause, as they do at country concerts when an artist launches into a favorite song. But the moment is slipping.

Lover…lover…lover…the word is echoing as if I was shouting it into a tin drum. Lover *is* the correct word. My mother always sang *husband*. God forbid that Sweet Betsy should have traveled about the country with a man she was not married to.

> With one yoke of oxen
> And an old yellow dog
> A tall Shanghai rooster
> And one spotted hog.

Those are the only words that will come to me, though I know there are a dozen verses to that old folk ballad. The song is called, I believe, *Sweet Betsy From Pike*. I repeat the words, my throat dry, my mouth feeling stuffed with dentist's cotton.

I can see swimming before me, a tableau of pioneer life: Sweet Betsy, Ike, oxen, rooster, dog, like a neatly choreographed scene from *How The West Was Won*. They wend their way across endless mountains and prairie. But the tableau is superimposed on a marriage license. Name of bride? Name of groom? Date of marriage?

The dark silhouettes of the audience comfort me as I begin the first verse of *Sweet Betsy From Pike* for the third time. It gives me a feeling of indescribable power. At the same time, I sense that they expect something else from me. But what? Why am I doing this?

Suddenly I see the why of it, and I feel light as a snowflake. I feel as if I have taken a hatchet and hacked from my ankles a shackling leaden shadow I have dragged behind me all my life. My singing is the first thing I have ever done just for me. Until now, I have spent my life painting bathing suits on nudes.

Over the music and the crowd murmur, I hear the small sputtering noises beginning in Zoltan's throat. "Uk, uk, uk." I stop what I am doing mid-word and move a step closer to Zoltan. I put my arm around his shoulders, find him rigid as a bookcase. I take a deep breath and begin again.

> Have you ever heard tell
> Of Sweet Betsy from Pike?

"Uk, uk, uk."

> Who crossed the wide mountains...

"Hoo crosst da wite moundains..." sings Zoltan, his voice as tinny and tuneless as mine. I grip his tense shoulder, try to pull him closer to me. Failing, I move myself closer to him until our shoulders touch.

I continue the song and Zoltan follows me, like a bad echo, repeating phonetically, gutturally, tonelessly, the words which are obviously strange to him. I glance toward Zoltan – we are both smiling, both 12 feet tall. I wonder what music it is he hears; if it is Greek, Yugoslav, Hungarian, or some other I cannot suspect. Is it happy music? Are there young dancers in festival costumes clattering through cobbled streets to its beat?

I know what I have to do. The next time Zoltan sings, I will join *him*. I will stand inflexible as he, honoring whatever invisible flag flutters in his mind.

> A tall Shanghai rooster
> And one spotted hog.

I sing.

As Zoltan finishes, I exhale, breathing out all the tension, terror and inadequacy. As I do, I feel Zoltan relax and suddenly his arm is around my waist and, grinning like mischievous children, we bow to the audience, as the applause like the beating of bird wings, rises and envelops us.

MOTHER TUCKER'S YELLOW DUCK

In August of 1968 we went to a concert in Vancouver – first panhandling spare change for the ferry ride and the entrance fee by working our way along Government Street and through Bastion Square, where the air was tangy with salt and the tourists clicked over the cobblestone in bright prints. I wonder if you remember that day, Glorianna, if you ever talk about it? Probably not. You live like a cat. As long as you're warm, well-fed, well-loved, you don't remember. You discard your days like soiled shirts, to be washed clean of the past, and returned to be used again.

The house is empty, Glorianna. The last bargain-hunter has carried off the last treasure, and I am alone with my footsteps. Carla insisted that I sell most of my furniture. "It will be cheaper to buy anything we need after we get settled than to pay to ship that junk from Victoria to Toronto," is what she said, and when I think of it I realize that I have sold all *my* furniture – what was *our* furniture, Glorianna. It is Carla's belongings that are being shipped to Toronto: the contents of her apartment, the chrome and glass coffee tables, the acre of waterbed, the white-pine kitchen table the color of honey, the deep, rust-colored sofa, soft as a plush-toy. And she is right, Glorianna. What I sold *was* junk. But it made me happy to see the young couples carting it away, exchanging secret smiles, so much in love, so full of hope. But now the house is empty and my footsteps follow me as if I am walking on a drum.

Somewhere, Glorianna, are you fending off questions? Waving them away like insects too close to your face. "You must have a past," someone will say to you, as I said to you so many times. But you'll smile sweetly, mysteriously, reach across the table for a cigarette, purse your lips as you exhale, and say nothing at all.

Carla has found us an apartment in Toronto. It is not far from Bloor Street, within walking distance of the university where I will be studying. The rent astounds me – parking costs as much as we once paid to rent this little house. But then I must remember that Carla earns a very substantial salary. She is already in Toronto, "Getting things organized," she says. When she phoned to tell me about the apartment, she mentioned, almost as an after-thought, that the management does not allow pets.

I've found a home for Hoover Shoats. The Writing Lady is going to adopt him. I guess you knew I'd look after him or you wouldn't have left him with me. He'll be happy with the Writing Lady. Carla is really not fond of cats. I used to wonder why you didn't take him with you. But I suppose I knew all along. Hoover Shoats is 12 years old, has rheumatism in one hip and eats only *Tender Vittles*. Hoover is here with me now, alone in the cooling house. I've left the bathroom window open a few inches so he can come in and sleep in the bathroom sink the way he likes. He may be able to do it for most of the summer: the Writing Lady's husband is going to remodel before he rents the house again.

After the concert it rained, that heavy, solid, stolid Vancouver summer rain. "Like having pails of water poured over our heads," you said. And we walked the streets of Gastown, staring in rain-bleary windows, and ducked into some of the ancient bars along E. Hastings Street, bars that smell like wet dogs, ashtrays, and spilled beer. We sat in a corner until a waiter or bouncer came along and told us to either buy a drink or leave. I guess I've lost my spirit of adventure, Glorianna, for now, 12 years later, I wouldn't even think of doing what we did then: traveling off to a strange city, knowing we had no place to sleep, no money for food, depending, as they say, on the kindness of strangers. But we were young and we didn't feel the cold. We slept on one of the hard, polished benches at the Bus Depot. I remained sitting up all night while you stretched out and used my lap as a pillow. You slept, scrunching up your eyes against the bright fluorescent lights, jumping once in a while as if you'd been touched by a live electric wire, saying "No," and "No, I won't," like a fretful child refusing to take medicine. We were soaked warm with love, Glorianna: you waking in the morning, your yellow hair smeared across your face, turning yourself to scratch your nose on my jeans, looking up at me with a smile so full of love.

"Did I talk?" you asked, as if in sleep you might have broken a promise or given away a secret of vital importance. What did you have to hide from me, Glorianna?

Outside in the brilliant sun, beside the dozing taxis, a man with a briefcase gave us two dollars. "I wish I had your nerve," he said, while you smiled your thanks and made the Peace Sign. Behind the taxis a bed of California poppies bloomed bright as egg yolks. You picked one and pushed its musky silk against my cheek. Glorianna, the house is so empty.

It was my aunt who got us this house though it was much against her better judgement to recommend us. "You keep it clean and pay the rent on time, Mac," she said to me four or five times. She was so afraid we'd embarrass her. The Writing Lady was a school friend of hers.

The Writing Lady and her husband have been next door all these years, in that huge white-frame house with the sunny study upstairs where she writes her novels. The Writing Lady always knew we weren't married, did I ever tell you that, Glorianna? "Your aunt mentioned how happily married you were so many times that I knew immediately you were probably happy but certainly not married." The Writing Lady misses you, Glorianna. She told me so. I was a bit afraid of her when we first moved here – so tall and statuesque, with her telephone-black hair and eyes – she used to come sweeping down her steps and across the lawn, her red-lined cape flapping. She reminded me of a Spanish dancer. And before I knew her well I imagined her playing the villain in a melodrama. She doesn't like Carla. Oh she never said so, but I can tell. I guess it is because Carla doesn't like this house.

The Writing Lady was a little horrified by you, in those early days, Glorianna – by the way you used to lounge on the front steps smoking, wearing only a halter and cutoff jeans, and by the way you painted daisies and black-eyed susans on one panel of the front door. Once, when I paid the rent she told me to ask you not to do that again. I never told you though, just hoped you wouldn't and you didn't.

We were standing in the yard a few days ago, the Writing Lady and I. Hoover was sitting on the step, paws tucked under him, looking scruffy as an old boot. The flowers on the door are so faded they look as if they've been painted over with milk. "Those were happy times weren't they, Mac," the Writing Lady said as she stared at the flowers. I know she was trying to tell me something.

I've spent most of the last few months at Carla's, just stopping here after classes for a change of clothes and to feed Hoover Shoats. Carla sniffed when she first came in this house. She didn't like the blankets we had for wall-hangings, or the hubcaps turning like mobiles in the living room, or the mattress on the floor in the bedroom. Hoover was asleep in the bathroom sink and opened one canary-colored eye about halfway and then closed it again. I wanted her to stay the night with me. "It's so much cozier at my place, don't you think?" she said, and I agreed with her.

I met Carla at the Business Management course I was taking when you left, Glorianna. She's an adult Probation Officer, but has plans to be a supervisor before long. The move to Toronto was her idea. "People on the coast have no sense of urgency," she says. She also thinks the university is better in the East, that my degree will carry more prestige and land me a better job. She says she spotted me right away as someone with drive and ambition. And she liked me for it. Liked me for wanting to improve myself. "Aren't you happy?" you used to ask whenever I suggested that I might get a full time job, that we might buy a house, a car, furniture. "Why?" you always said, your hands loving, your eyes the perfect blue of a television backdrop.

Remember how, just a few days after we moved into this house, a girl with daffodils braided into her long chestnut hair, brought a box of kittens into the bar of the Churchill Hotel. I think that is the only thing you ever asked me for, and you did it in silence, with just a look. I nodded, and you picked up a kitten, a tiny bleating thing, its eyes barely open. I named him Hoover Shoats, after an evangelist and false prophet in a novel by Flannery O'Connor. You never questioned where the name came from, just held him cupped in the palm of one hand only a thin blue workshirt between him and the warmth of your breast. Later, I went out and bought a small carton of milk, got a clean ashtray from the bar, and Hoover Shoats stood all wobbly-kneed on the green terrycloth table top, and lapped milk with his tiny raspberry tongue. He was surrounded by beer glasses, as if in a magical forest of amber and crystal trees.

"Do you have a last name?" I asked, after we had been together for several days. Courtships are usually two separate monologues. I was discovering that ours was one, mine. You were loving and cheerful and happy, but your talk was only of today.

"Why do I need a last name?" you asked, answering my question with a question, something I was beginning to notice you did frequently. We were sitting on a bench in Beacon Hill Park, trellices of roses nearby, your head on my shoulder, your fingers with their wide, pale nails exploring my arm.

"What if you wanted to open a bank account?"

"I don't need one."

"What if someone gave you a check? You'd have to sign it."

"People I know don't write checks."

"The hospital," I cried triumphantly. "What if you get really sick? They won't admit someone without a name."

"I'd pretend to be unconscious," you said, slumping against me.

"Seriously."

"Seriously. Initial I., Glorianna," you said, and smiled maddeningly.

"You can't discard your past as easily as a playing card," I insisted, but you only looked at me with your languid, half-amused smile, your blue-ribbon colored eyes.

I never knew how old you were, Glorianna. That day we met on the street in front of the Cool Aid Hostel, your hair the color of lemon pie, laying in swatches across your bare shoulders, your faded jeans patched with squares of red flannel, making you look like a walking semaphore message, you might have been 14 or 18, or 22. You might have run away from your parents, or from a high school where you were a cheerleader, or from your own husband and child.

"How old are you?" I asked, when we'd known each other no more than an hour. But you turned your lower lip out and down and said, "What is time anyway?" And later you made me take off my wristwatch and carry it in my pocket, though you wanted me to give it away.

"Push time as far away as you can," you said, holding your hands up in front of you as if pushing on an invisible wall.

"Who are you and where do you come from?" I insisted.

"Do you like me?" you asked, and turned your face up to be kissed. And I did kiss you, not noticing then that my questions always went unanswered.

Glorianna, I wish that I might shed my skin like a snake, leave it crinkling in the sun, and never think of it again. But my past clings to me, like crawly things drawn to me for my warmth.

"Our past is tied to us, like tin cans and old shoes to a wedding car," I said to you once. "It rattles and bumps behind us in a ragtag tangle of uselessness."

"Not mine," you replied, with your slow-curving, innocent smile.

The Cool Aid Hostel is still there, Glorianna, though it is a quiet place now: late at night the police drop off old winos at the front door. The hostel caters to derelicts now, or to young couples with huge back-packs, and checkbooks, wearing $200 boots. Not like when we met. Not like that sweet-smelling spring when the streets of Victoria were inch deep in cherry blossoms. Not like that wondrous, ephemeral summer when, like animals that migrate every so many years, young people poured out across the land, owning only their clothes; with a turned out thumb, and a smile and the phrase "spare change" lighting their way. They flooded forth thousands strong to the beat of soft music, surrounded by an aura of love.

That first day, as we sat in the sun and talked, you emptied your pockets of half a book of matches, and a ratty pink comb with many teeth missing.

"That's all?" I asked incredulously.

"I'm here. Why do I need to bring anything with me?" you said.

I showed you my wallet, full of photos and identification pieces, thought of the $10 stashed in my boot.

Even Charlie Barber, the man who founded Cool Aid, wears a suit now, Glorianna. I suppose you disapprove of the changes in his life as much as you disapprove of the changes in mine. Cool Aid was his child and he fought for it like a mother bird defending her nest. Charlie: slim, denimed, bearded, with flint-like eyes and the ability to conjure and cajole money, food, blankets, or medical supplies, all seemingly out of empty pavement.

Remember how we used to hang around the back door of that

Italian restaurant, Glorianna? And how they saved the uneaten slices of pizza for us, put them into a green plastic bag, and we'd trip back to Cool Aid, holding hands and swinging the bag between us as parents might swing a child. Then we'd sit around and feast. And Charlie would praise us.

Charlie wears a suit and tie and sits in the legislature. He still defends the poor and still loses more than he wins, for the province is governed by car dealers who stymie the social programs Charlie and his party try to introduce.

The band we went to see in Vancouver was Mother Tucker's Yellow Duck. I remember them mainly because of their name, not their music. We sat on the cool soft grass on a sidehill 50 yards from the bandshell. And we openly smoked-up. Almost everyone did, feeling very daring and rebellious. You were barefoot, Glorianna, and you picked dandelions and put one between each of your toes...

I saw one of the band members a few weeks ago, walking across Bastion Square, where the tourists still flutter through like flags. There are only tourists and business people now, but I could still see the shadows of the ragged, denimed kids of the late 60s who so genially panhandled. Our ghosts were there, Glorianna, like black and white photographs. Sometimes I wish I were with you, wherever you are, wish that I hadn't turned in my credentials, whatever they were. But I look at myself: Carla has bought me Pierre Cardin shirts and stylish corduroy slacks. "I want you to make a good impression at university," she says. "You never know who'll be able to help you with your career later on." And I let her do and say these things... Are you in your sleeping bag on someone's floor this morning, Glorianna, your jeans and red-checkered shirt sprawled nearby?

The band member was swathed in a $400 business suit, his neck constricted by a silk tie; his hair was immaculately styled, an inch or two longer that the colleagues who accompanied him. His concession to the past. He was probably a lawyer, stockbroker, or

accountant. But I remember him in that sun-warmed park, slamming out his music like a power-hitter belting home runs, shirtless,
glistening with sweat, wild-eyed, his hair a fuzzy halo around his
gaunt face.

After we settled into the house, I worked for awhile for that
leather shop downstairs in Bastion Square, called *Golden Apples of
the Sun*, and the mouthwatering odors of tanned leather used to
cling to my clothes. Those days, Glorianna, you would sit around
in Bastion Square, lounge near the old anchor which is whitewashed to the pearly color of doves, play a few notes on your
guitar, lay a square silk handkerchief, patterned with a wondrous
mandala, on the cobblestones, weighing down each corner with a
tiny, polished rock, and watch the cache of quarters grow as the
easygoing tourists emptied their pockets.

"Oh, you smell like a swatch of buckskin," you'd say to me
when I came out to join you at lunch hour, and you'd rub your nose
against my chest. "You must be an Indian," you'd go on. "I bet you
could be an Indian. See how dark your arms are. Your profile is
Indian too, your nose is straight, and your brow high and noble,"
and you'd kiss me and press your belly up against mine, and not
care who was watching, your hair smelling tangy as the crisp
ocean breeze that tousled it.

Carla's house here in Victoria is sold. As soon as we get
organized in Toronto, she wants to buy an acre or two in the
country and build an A-frame. Carla is used to earning good
money. She owned a house in Toronto, one she came away with
when she divorced her husband. She sold it when she came to
Victoria and put a large down payment on a newly renovated
house, close to downtown but still in a residential area. She lived
alone. One bedroom was a sewing room, another a study. When I
first knew her I suggested she should rent those rooms to university
students. "You could share the kitchen with them," I said. Carla
looked at me as if I were a child. "It would help with the mortgage
payments," I went on.

"Mac, if you have a good job you don't need help with your mortgage payments," she replied.

I realized then that though I was 30 years old, I'd never earned $5,000 in a year.

Carla has a microwave oven. Her house, despite the sharp angles of the chrome lamp poles, was pleasant but organized: plants hung in macramé slings, the rooms were decorated with dishes Carla had made herself. At this moment, all these posses-sions are on their way to Toronto, cushioned like eggs in a rectangular orange semitrailer.

One evening, Glorianna, on the spur of the moment, I took my only photo of you: one in which you are wearing jeans and a lemon-colored sweater and smiling mysteriously, pushing your breasts toward the camera in response to some joke I have made, and I went to Bastion Square. I walked down the long, steep flight of beery-smelling stairs to the Churchill Hotel Bar. It is now called the Bastion Inn, but the change of name has never taken place in my head. The freaks still hang out there, Glorianna, the few that are left. There were perhaps 10 tables of long-haired, denimed youngsters, sprawled with their feet deliberately blocking the aisles, or sitting up straight, earnestly arguing, their faces sincere and urgent. They looked like we did when we met, Glorianna, and I felt so old. I walked from table to table showing your picture, asking if they'd seen you. I got virtually no response and I realized as I was leaving, trudging back up the gritty steps, that it was because of the way I looked. My hair was too short, too well styled, my shirt and shoes too expensive, my jeans too new. And the watch Carla had given me sat on my wrist glowing like a square inch of chrome. There was actually hostility in some of the faces that dismissed me. They may have even thought I was a cop, or a wristwatch hippie... I wonder if they still use that term. But there was something else, Glorianna, a meanness, a hardness that wasn't there in our time, and I wonder if you have been able to fit back in to that kind of life.

Until that evening I really thought of going into the dope-and-denim bars of Victoria and Vancouver and seriously searching for you, or a shadow of you. I thought of settling for someone like you, someone street-wise, but happy, easy, loving. But as I stared at those hard young faces I realized that it is almost impossible to live in more than one generation at a time. I think of Carla and vibrate with anticipation of accomplishing something.

Glorianna, do you remember how, in the mornings, the cats used to sit in the sun on the big, east-facing doorstep of the Writing Lady's house? Do you remember the way they sat, paws tucked under them, sunning themselves like old men swathed in blankets: McKenzie, the Writing Lady's cat, and our Hoover Shoats. McKenzie died of old age a few months ago: that scruffy old thug of a cat with his frost-bitten ears and fight scarred face. When he got too sick, the Writing Lady carried him off to the vet's, carried him in an apple box, and him all wrapped up like a doll. "The vet put him to sleep," the Writing Lady said.

We just rolled along, Glorianna. What we had was good enough for you, always. But there were nameless fears that walked in my blood and I felt that one day I'd wake up, old as McKenzie and Hoover Shoats, and find I had spent my life sunning myself.

"You worry too much," you said. "We'll always get by." And we did. I showed you how I made belts and watchbands, and you said, "I can do that too," and you did. "Why go out every day when you can stay home?" you said, and I set up a workbench in the tiny basement, and we discovered that with only a few hours work a week we would earn enough to exist. Existing has always been enough for you.

"What are we going to do when we're 50?" I demanded of you once.

"Why?" was all you could say in reply. Then after a pause, "I don't think about it. Why can't you just let life happen to you?"

But I couldn't, could I, Glorianna? And I could never adequately explain why I began taking courses, or why I continued.

The first one was just curiosity, to see if I could really do work at the college level. But I found it easy – I rolled over the other students like a professional halfback in a high school game. I read 10 times what was required for every course I took. The other students were so lazy, so careless, so unmotivated. Desire for learning fell on me like a disease: I was ravenous for knowledge.

"Why worry about tomorrow?" you said. "What do you see in the mirror that I don't?"

"What if the Writing Lady sells this house? They're talking about retiring, you know. Where would we live?"

"We could go back on the street for awhile. There's always some place to crash," you said. But I always feel sad when I see those ageing hippies, in bars or sitting on park benches, dressed and looking just as they did a decade earlier except for the lines of age on their faces and hands.

"But what about Hoover?" I said, realizing the instant I said it how ridiculous it sounded.

"We'll beg spare change to buy him cat food. I'll teach him to pick a few notes on my guitar. I'll dress him up in doll clothes, the old ladies will love it."

"I see the age in my eyes," I said.

Then, Glorianna, you smiled with your wondrous red lips, and though remaining perfectly still moved another step away from me. I could have stopped you anytime. Why didn't I? Why did I insist on you meeting Carla, on us visiting her home. Watching you drift away was like staring at a glistening cast-iron pump handle on a frosty morning – knowing that sticking my tongue on it would bring me pain but being unable to resist.

Glorianna, I'm like a guerrilla soldier who's been living in the jungle for years not knowing the war is over. I emerge, thin, ragged and uncomprehending. My comrades have won the war and are all generals and ambassadors doing all the things we fought to destroy. I learn that there is already a small, new, group of insurgents in the hills plotting another overthrow of another government. As I look around I know I would be better off to seek out the insurgents. But I don't. I turn my gun in for a briefcase, my ragged uniform for a business suit, my integrity for an indexed pension plan.

It was Carla's energy that attracted me to her. She was taking an accounting course for the sheer joy of learning. Carla is always moving, nervous, watchful, like a penned animal, pacing back and forth endlessly, never tiring.

When I came to sell the household goods I realized that they were all mine alone, or things we had acquired together, Glorianna. There was nothing of yours. You left nothing behind you. Yet you took nothing with you. You might never have existed.

Carla is real. She has parents: her father a lawyer in Ottawa, her mother a wilted flower who uses religion as a rubber crutch to get from psychiatrist to psychiatrist. She has a sister who lost a hand in a car accident, and a brother with a mysterious disease that requires him to ingest large quantities of cortisone. In her house, Carla had her high school yearbooks, all her ex-husband's love letters, and a copy of a letter she wrote her parents on her 21st birthday, thanking and praising them for the way they had raised her.

Yet I think of the way we loved, Glorianna. "Move slowly," you said, and your tongue would move like a butterfly inside my mouth. "Pretend we're water and in a while we'll be all mixed together so warm and so wet…"

I didn't know how to react when you told me you were leaving. I could see that things were going to get worse between us. But anyone else would have stayed…longer.

"It's what you really want," you said. "It will only be a tragedy if you make it one." And then you smiled sadly. "I think you'll change your mind in a while," you added.

"Then what?" I said.

"Then you'll have to look around for someone more like me."

"Carla and I are only friends," I protested. And it was true. But

I suppose I had used her as an example, thrown her name out, like a dart, too many times.

"Then neither of us have anything to feel bad about," you said. "You're not meant to be closed in, Mac," and you pointed your enigmatic smile at me again. "Melmac, ceramic, macramé, micro-wave," you intoned, the smile never leaving your face.

The Writing Lady is going to adopt Hoover Shoats. He's practically been living with her these past few months and she likes it, she says. He sleeps in the sun, on a cushion on a rocking chair in that big, warm upstairs where she writes her novels. It will be a great place for him to spend his old age.

I check the basement before I leave for good; it is hollow down here too, nothing left but the flyspecked fluorescent tubes above where the workbench used to be. I look all around to be certain I've forgotten nothing, am about to leave when a minute movement catches my eye, and I notice hanging high above the workbench, samples of our art. There are a half-dozen watchbands dangling from a plumbing pipe, various lengths of tooled leather, each strap coming to a point like a spike, each suspended in mid-air by a frail thread. The bands are spaced at about six-inch intervals and look like pieces of a mobile. Something, probably my displacing the air currents, caused one of them to spin lazily, catching my eye. I realize that I don't own one of my own watch straps. As a concession to you, Glorianna, I haven't worn a watch in years, until Carla gave me this one: a thin silver wafer with lights that blink and alarms that squawk demandingly, attached to my wrist by a lustrous silver bracelet, fine as a shaving head.

I am standing directly below the row of watch bands, neck bent back, my breath has started them all moving, twisting and turning slowly as corpses. These six little lengths of leather are all that is left of our lives together, Glorianna. You and I, Mother Tucker's Yellow Duck, Charlie Barber, Hoover Shoats, the Writing Lady, all twisting helplessly in mid-air.

I reach up, grab one and pull, but it is tenacious and the waxy thread cuts into my fingers. As I release it, it bucks and twirls wildly. I take out my pocket knife and one by one, like cutting flowers for a bouquet, sever the threads and lay the bands side by side on the flat of my hand, the limp strings dangling.

ABOUT THE AUTHOR

W. P. Kinsella has published 15 books and over 200 short stories; he is best known for his multi-award-winning novel, **Shoeless Joe**, which became the movie **Field of Dreams** in 1989. Other books include **Dance Me Outside, The Iowa Baseball Confederacy, The Thrill of the Grass**, and **The Fencepost Chronicles**, which won the Leacock Medal for Humor in 1987. His most recent books are **The Miss Hobbema Pageant**, a new collection of stories about Frank Fencepost and his friends, and a book of poetry, **The Rainbow Warehouse**, co-authored with his wife, Ann Knight.

Born in Edmonton, Alberta, Kinsella earned a B.A. at the University of Victoria in 1974 and an M.F.A. at the University of Iowa in 1978. He and his wife now live in White Rock, British Columbia, and he also spends time in Iowa City, Iowa.